In a small jungle-fring̲ ̲ ̲ ̲ ̲ ̲ ̲ ̲ ̲ ̲ ̲ ̲ ̲ ̲ ̲ ̲ ̲ ̲ ̲
men who were not men faced a ninth. All wore the
cyanotic blue skins of Venus, though only three had
been born with those skins. The others were surgical
products, Earthmen converted to Venusians. Not
just their bodies had been converted, either. The six
changed ones had all been Vorsters at one time in
their spiritual development.

The Vorsters were the most powerful figures on
Earth. But this was not Earth but Venus, and Venus
was in the hands of the Harmonists, sometimes called
the Lazarites after their martyred founder, David
Lazarus. Lazarus, the prophet of Transcendent Harmony, had been put to death by Vorster underlings
more than sixty years before . . .

"What turned up on Mars doesn't tally with the
myth," the ninth man, Mondschein, was saying.
"Lazarus isn't *supposed* to be resurrected in the
flesh. He was blasted to atoms. Suppose archaeologists found that Christ had really been beheaded, not
crucified. Suppose it came to light that Mohammed
never set foot in Mecca? We've been caught with our
mythology askew. If this really is Lazarus, it could
destroy us. It could wreck all we've built . . . ."

TO OPEN THE SKY

Robert Silverberg

BANTAM BOOKS
TORONTO • NEW YORK • LONDON • SYDNEY • AUCKLAND

TO OPEN THE SKY
*A Bantam Book / published by arrangement with
the Author*

Bantam edition / December 1984

All rights reserved.
Copyright © 1967 by Robert Silverberg.
Cover artwork copyright © 1984 by Jim Burns.
*This book may not be reproduced in whole or in part, by
mimeograph or any other means, without permission.*
For information address: Bantam Books, Inc.

ISBN 0-553-24502-3

Published simultaneously in the United States and Canada

PRINTED IN THE UNITED STATES OF AMERICA

H   0 9 8 7 6 5 4 3 2 1

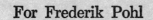
For Frederik Pohl

ONE

Blue Fire
2077

THE ELECTROMAGNETIC LITANY

Stations of the Spectrum

And there is light, before and beyond our vision, for which we give thanks.

And there is heat, for which we are humble.

And there is power, for which we count ourselves blessed.

Blessed be Balmer, who gave us our wavelengths.
Blessed be Bohr, who brought us understanding.
Blessed be Lyman, who saw beyond sight.

Tell us now the stations of the spectrum.

Blessed be long radio waves, which oscillate slowly.

Blessed be broadcast waves, for which we thank Hertz.

Blessed be short waves, linkers of mankind, and blessed be microwaves.

Blessed be infrared, bearers of nourishing heat.

Blessed be visible light, magnificent in angstroms. (*On high holidays only:* Blessed be red, sacred to Doppler. Blessed be orange. Blessed be yellow, hallowed by Fraunhofer's gaze. Blessed be green. Blessed be blue for its hydrogen line. Blessed be indigo. Blessed be violet, flourishing with energy.)

Blessed be ultraviolet, with the richness of the sun.

Blessed be X rays, sacred to Roentgen, the prober within.

Blessed be the gamma, in all its power; blessed be the highest of frequencies.

We give thanks for Planck. We give thanks for Einstein. We give thanks in the highest for Maxwell.

In the strength of the spectrum, the quantum, and the holy angstrom, peace!

one

There was chaos on the face of the earth, but to the man in the Nothing Chamber it did not matter.

Ten billion people—or was it twelve billion by now?—fought for their place in the sun. Skyscrapers shot heavenward like sprouting beanstalks. The Martians mocked. The Venusians spat. Nut-cults flourished, and in a thousand cells the Vorsters bowed low to their devilish blue glow. All of this, at the moment, was of no significance to Reynolds Kirby. He was out of it. He was the man in the Nothing Chamber.

The place of his repose was four thousand feet above the blue Caribbean, in his hundredth-story apartment on Tortola in the Virgin Islands. A man had to take his rest somewhere. Kirby, as a high official in the U.N., had the right to warmth and slumber, and a substantial chunk of his salary covered the overhead on this hideaway. The building was a tower of shining glass whose foundations drove deep into the heart of the island. One could not build a skyscraper like this on every Caribbean island; too many of them were flat disks of dead coral, lacking the substance to support half a million tons of deadweight. Tortola was different, a retired volcano, a submerged mountain. Here they could build, and here they had built.

Reynolds Kirby slept the good sleep.

Half an hour in a Nothing Chamber restored a man to vitality, draining the poisons of fatigue from his body and mind. Three hours in it left him limp, flaccid-willed. A twenty-four-hour stint could make any man a puppet. Kirby lay in a warm nutrient bath, ears plugged, eyes capped, feed-lines bringing air to his lungs. There was nothing like crawling back into the womb for a while when the world was too much with you.

The minutes ticked by. Kirby did not think of Vorsters. Kirby did not think of Nat Weiner, the Martian. Kirby did not think of the esper girl, writhing in her bed of torment, whom he had seen in Kyoto last week. Kirby did not think.

A voice purred, "Are you ready, Freeman Kirby?"

Kirby was not ready. Who ever was? A man had to be driven from his Nothing Chamber by an angel with a flaming sword. The nutrient bath began to bubble out of the tank. Rubber-cushioned metal fingers peeled the caps from his eyeballs. His ears were unplugged. Kirby lay shivering for a moment, expelled from the womb, resisting the return to reality. The chamber's cycle was complete; it could not be turned on again for twenty-four hours, and a good thing, too.

"Did you sleep well, Freeman Kirby?"

Kirby scowled rustily and clambered to his feet. He swayed, nearly lost his balance, but the robot servitor was there to steady him. Kirby caught a burnished arm and held it until the spasm passed.

"I slept marvelously well," he told the metal creature. "It's a pity to return."

"You don't mean that, Freeman. You know that the only true pleasure comes from an engagement with life. You said that to me yourself, Freeman Kirby."

"I suppose I did," Kirby admitted dryly. All of the robot's pious philosophy stemmed from things he had said. He accepted a robe from the squat, flat-faced thing and pulled it over his shoulders. He shivered again. Kirby was a lean man, too tall for his weight, with stringy, corded arms and legs, close-cropped gray hair, deep-set greenish eyes. He was forty, and looked fifty, and before climbing into the Nothing Chamber today he had felt about seventy.

"When does the Martian arrive?" he asked.

"Seventeen hours. He's at a banquet in San Juan right now, but he'll be along soon."

"I can't wait," Kirby said. Moodily he moved to the nearest window and depolarized it. He looked down, way down, at the tranquil water lapping at the beach. He could see the dark line of the coral reef, green water on the hither side, deep blue water beyond. The reef was dead, of course. The delicate creatures who had built it could stand only so much motor fuel in their systems, and the level of tolerance had been passed quite some time ago. The skittering hydrofoils buzzing from island to island left a trail of murderous slime in their wake.

The U.N. man closed his eyes. And opened them quickly, for when he lowered the lids there appeared on the screen of his brain the sight of that esper girl again, twisting, screaming, biting her knuckles, yellow skin flecked with gleaming beads of sweat. And the Vorster man standing by, waving that damned blue glow around, murmuring, "Peace, child, peace, you will soon be in harmony with the All."

That had been last Thursday. This was the following Wednesday. She was in harmony with the All by now, Kirby thought, and an irreplaceable pool of genes had been scattered to the four winds. Or the seven winds. He was having trouble keeping his clichés straight these days.

Seven seas, he thought. *Four winds.*

The shadow of a copter crossed his line of sight.

"Your guest is arriving," the robot declared.

"Magnificent," Kirby said sourly.

The news that the Martian was on hand set Kirby jangling with tension. He had been selected as the guide, mentor, and watchdog for the visitor from the Martian colony. A great deal depended on maintaining friendly relations with the Martians, for they represented markets vital to Earth's economy. They also represented vigor and drive, commodities currently in short supply on Earth.

But they were also a headache to handle—touchy, mercurial, unpredictable. Kirby knew that he had a big job on his hands. He had to keep the Martian out of harm's way, coddle him and cosset him, all without ever seeming patronizing or oversolicitous. And if Kirby bungled it—well, it could be costly to Earth and fatal to Kirby's own career.

He opaqued the window again and hurried into his bedroom to change into robes of state. A clinging gray tunic, green foulard, boots of blue leather, gloves of gleaming golden mesh—he looked every inch the important Earthside official by the time the annunciator clanged to inform him that Nathaniel Weiner of Mars had come to call.

"Show him in," Kirby said.

The door irised open, and the Martian stepped nimbly through. He was a small, compact man in his early thirties, unnaturally wide-shouldered, with thin lips, jutting cheekbones, dark beady eyes. He looked physically powerful, as though he had spent his life struggling with the killing gravity of Jupiter, not romping in the airy effortlessness of Mars. He was deeply tanned, and a fine network of wrinkles radiated from the corners of his eyes. He looked aggressive, thought Kirby. He looked arrogant.

"Freeman Kirby, it's a pleasure to see you," the Martian said in a deep, rasping voice.

"The honor is mine, Freeman Weiner."

"Permit me," Weiner said. He drew his laser pistol. Kirby's robot scurried forward with the velvet cushion. The Martian placed the weapon carefully on the plush mound. The robot slid across the floor to bring the gun to Kirby.

"Call me Nat," the Martian said.

Kirby smiled thinly. He picked up the gun, resisted the insane temptation to ash the Martian on the spot, and briefly examined it. Then he replaced it on the cushion and flicked his hand at the robot, who carried it back to its owner.

"My friends call me Ron," Kirby said. "Reynolds is a lousy first name."

"Glad to know you, Ron. What's to drink?"

Kirby was jarred by the breach of etiquette, but he

maintained an equable diplomatic mask. The Martian had been punctilious enough with his gun ritual, but you'd expect that with any frontiersman; it didn't mean that his manners extended beyond that. Smoothly Kirby said, "Whatever you like, Nat. Synthetics, realies—you name it and it's here. What about a filtered rum?"

"I've had so much rum I'm ready to puke it, Ron. Those gabogos in San Juan drink it like water. What about some decent whiskey?"

"You dial it," Kirby said with a grand sweep of his hand. The robot picked up the console of the bar and carried it to the Martian. Weiner eyed the buttons a moment and stabbed almost at random, twice.

"I'm ordering a double rye for you," Weiner announced. "And a double bourbon for me."

Kirby found that amusing. The rude colonial was not only selecting his own drink but one for his host. Double rye, indeed! Kirby hid his wince and took the drink. Weiner slipped comfortably into a webfoam cradle. Kirby sat also.

"How are you enjoying your visit to Earth?" Kirby asked.

"Not bad. Not bad. Sickening the way you people are crammed together here, though."

"It's the human condition."

"Not on Mars it isn't. Not on Venus, either."

"Give it time," Kirby said.

"I doubt it. We know how to regulate our population up there, Ron."

"So do we. It just took us a while to get the idea across to everybody, and by that time there were ten billion of us. We hope to keep the rate of increase down."

"You know what?" Weiner said. "You ought to take every tenth person and feed 'em to the converters. Get some good energy back out of all that meat. Cut your population by a billion overnight." He chuckled. "Not serious. Wouldn't be ethical. Just a passing joke."

Kirby smiled. "You aren't the first to suggest it, Nat. And some of the others were plenty serious."

"Discipline—that's the answer to every human problem. Discipline and more self-discipline. Denial. Planning. This whiskey is damned good, Ron. How about another round?"

"Help yourself."

Weiner did. Generously.

"Damned fine stuff," he murmured. "We don't get drinks like this on Mars. Got to admit it, Ron. Crowded and stinking as this planet is, it's got comforts. I wouldn't want to live here, mind you, but I'm glad I came. The women—mmmm! The drinks! The excitement!"

"You've been here two days?" Kirby asked.

"That's right. One night in New York—ceremonies, banquet, all that garbage, sponsored by the Colonial Association. Then down to Washington to see the President. Nice old chap. Soft belly, though. Could stand some exercise. Then this idiot thing in San Juan, a day of hospitality, meeting the Puerto Rican comrades, that kind of junk. And now here. What's to do here, Ron?"

"Well, we could go downstairs for a swim first—"

"I can swim all I like on Mars. I want to see civilization, not water. Complexity." Weiner's eyes glowed. Kirby abruptly realized that the man had been drunk when he walked in and that the two stiff jolts of bourbon had sent him into a fine glow of intoxication. "You know what I want to do, Kirby? I want to get out and grub in the dirt a little. I want to go to opium dens. I want to see espers have ecstasies. I want to take in a Vorster session. I want to live the life, Ron. I want to experience Earth—muck and all!"

two

The Vorster hall was in a shabby, almost intolerably seedy old building in central Manhattan, practically within spitting distance of the U.N. buildings. Kirby felt queasy about entering it; he had never really conquered his uneasiness about slumming, even now when most of the world was one vast teeming slum. But Nat Weiner had commanded it, and so it must be. Kirby had brought him here because it was the only Vorster place he had visited before, and so he didn't feel too sharply out of place among the worshipers.

The sign over the door said in glowing but splotchy letters:

BROTHERHOOD OF THE IMMANENT RADIANCE
ALL WELCOME
SERVICES DAILY
HEAL YOUR HEARTS
HARMONIZE WITH THE ALL

Weiner snickered at the sign. "Look at that! Heal your hearts! How's your heart, Kirby?"

"Punctured in several places. Shall we go in?"

"You bet we shall," Weiner said.

The Martian was sloshingly drunk. He held his liquor well, Kirby had to admit. Through the long evening Kirby had not even tried to match the colonial envoy drink for drink, and yet he felt hazy and overheated. The tip of his nose prickled. He yearned to shake Weiner off and crawl back into the Nothing Chamber to get all this poison out of his system.

But Weiner wanted to kick over the traces, and it was hard to blame him for that. Mars was a rough place, where there was no time for self-indulgence. Terraforming a planet took a maximum effort. The job was nearly done now, after two generations of toil, and the air of Mars was sweet and clean, but no one was relaxing up there yet. Weiner was here to negotiate a trade agreement, but it was also his first chance to escape from the rigors of Martian life. The Sparta of space, they called it. And here he was in Athens.

They entered the Vorster hall.

It was long and narrow, an oblong box of a room. A dozen rows of unpainted wooden benches ran from wall to wall, with a narrow aisle down one side. At the rear was the altar, glowing with the inevitable blue radiance. Behind it stood a tall, skeleton-thin man, bald, bearded.

"Is that the priest?" Weiner whispered harshly.

"I don't think they're called priests," said Kirby. "But he's in charge."

"Do we take communion?"

"Let's just watch," Kirby suggested.

"Look at all these damned maniacs," the Martian said.

"This is a very popular religious movement."

"I don't get it."

"Watch. Listen."

"Down on their knees—groveling to that half-pint reactor—"

Heads were turning in their direction. Kirby sighed. He had no love for the Vorsters or their religion himself, but he was embarrassed at this boisterous desecration of their shrine. Most undiplomatically, he took Weiner's arm, guided the Martian into the nearest pew, and pulled him down into a kneeling position. Kirby knelt beside him. The Martian gave him an ugly glance. Colonists didn't like their bodies handled by strangers. A Venusian might have slashed at Kirby with his dagger for something like that. But, then, a Venusian wouldn't be here on Earth at all, let alone cutting capers in a Vorster hall.

Sullenly, Weiner grabbed the rail and leaned forward to watch the service. Kirby squinted through the near darkness at the man behind the altar.

The reactor was on and glowing—a cube of cobalt-60, shielded by water, the dangerous radiations gobbled up before they could sear through flesh. In the darkness Kirby saw a faint blue glow, rising slowly in brightness, growing more intense. Now the lattice of the tiny reactor was masked in whitish-blue light, and around it swirled a weird greenish-blue glow that seemed almost purple at its core. It was the Blue Fire, the eerie cold light of the Cerenkov radiation, spreading outward to envelop the entire room.

It was nothing mystical, Kirby knew. Electrons were surging through that tank of water, moving at a velocity greater than light in that medium, and as they moved they hurled forth a stream of photons. There were neat equations to explain the source of the Blue Fire. Give the Vorsters credit: they didn't say it was anything supernatural. But it made a useful symbolic instrument, a focus for religious emotions, more colorful than a crucifix, more dramatic than the Tables of the Law.

The Vorster up front said quietly, "There is a Oneness from which all life stems. The infinite variety of the universe we owe to the motion of the electrons. Atoms meet; their particles entwine. Electrons leap from orbit to orbit, and chemical changes are worked."

"Listen to the pious bastard," Weiner snorted. "A chemistry lecture, yet!"

Kirby bit his lip in anguish. A girl in the pew just in front of theirs turned around and said in a low, urgent voice, "Please. Please—just listen."

She was such a numbing sight that even Weiner was struck dumb for once. The Martian gasped in shock. Kirby, who had seen surgically altered women before, scarcely reacted at all. Iridescent cups covered the openings where her ears had been. An opal was mounted in the bone of her forehead. Her eyelids were of gleaming foil.

The surgeons had done things to her nostrils, to her lips. Perhaps she had been in some terrible accident. More likely she had had herself maimed for cosmetic purposes. Madness. Madness.

The Vorster said, "The energy of the sun—the green life surging in plants—the bursting wonder of growth—for this we thank the electron. The enzymes of our body—the sparking synapses of our brains—the beating of our hearts—for this we thank the electron. Fuel and food, light and heat, warmth and nourishment, everything and all, rising from the Oneness, rising from the Immanent Radiance—"

It was a litany, Kirby realized. All around him people were swaying in rhythm with the half-chanted words, were nodding, even weeping. The Blue Fire swelled and reached to the sagging ceiling. The man at the altar raised his long, spidery arms in a kind of benediction.

"Come forward," he cried. "Come kneel and join in praise! Lock arms, bow heads, give thanks for the underlying unity of all things!"

The Vorsters began to shamble toward the altar. It woke memories of an Episcopalian childhood for Kirby: going forward to take communion, the wafer on the tongue, the quick sip of wine, the smell of incense, the rustle of priestly robes. He hadn't been to a service in twenty-five years. It was a long way from the vaulted magnificence of the cathedral to the dilapidated ugliness of this improvised shrine, but for a moment Kirby felt a flicker of religious feeling, felt just the faintest urge to move foward with the others and kneel before the glowing reactor.

The thought stunned and shocked him.

How had it stolen upon him? This was no religion. This was cultism, a wildfire movement, the latest fad, here today, gone tomorrow. Ten million converts overnight? What of it? Tomorrow or the next day would come the newest prophet, exhorting the faithful to plunge their hands into a scintillation counter's sparkling bath, and the Vorster halls would be deserted. This was no Rock. This was quicksand.

And yet there had been that momentary pull—

Kirby tightened his lips. It was the strain, he thought, of shepherding this wild Martian around all evening. He didn't give a damn for the supernal Oneness. The underlying unity of all things meant nothing to him. This was a place for the tired, the neurotic, the novelty-hungry, for the kind of person that would cheerfully pay good money to have her ears cut off and her nostrils slit. It was a measure of his own desperation that he had been almost ready to join the communicants at the altar.

He relaxed.

And in the same moment Nat Weiner burst to his feet and went careening down the aisle.

"Save me!" the Martian cried. "Heal my goddam soul! Show me the Oneness!"

"Kneel with us, Brother," the Vorster leader said smoothly.

"I'm a sinner!" Weiner howled. "I'm full of booze and corruption! I got to be saved! I embrace the electron! I yield!"

Kirby hurried after him down the aisle. Was Weiner serious? The Martians were notorious for their resistance to any and all religious movements, including the established and legitimate ones. Had he somehow succumbed to that hellish blue glow?

"Take the hands of your brethren," the leader murmured. "Bow your head and let the glow enfold you."

Weiner looked to his left. The girl with the surgical alterations knelt beside him. She held out her hand. Four fingers of flesh, one of some turquoise-hued metal.

"It's a monster!" Weiner shrieked. "Take it away! I won't let you cut me up!"

"Be calm, Brother—"

"You're a bunch of phonies! Phonies! Phonies! Phonies! Nothing but a pack of—"

Kirby got to him. He dug his fingertips into the ridged muscles of Weiner's back in a way that the Martian was likely to notice, drunk as he was.

In a low, intense voice Kirby said, "Let's go, Nat. We're getting out of here."

"Take your stinking hands off me, Earther!"

"Nat, please—this is a house of worship—"

"This is a bughouse! Crazy! Crazy! Crazy! Look at them! Down on their knees like stinking maniacs!" Weiner struggled to his feet. His booming voice seemed to batter at the walls. "I'm a free man from Mars! I dug in the desert with these hands! I watched the oceans fill! What did any of you do? You cut your eyelids off and wallowed in muck! And you—you fake priest, you take their money and love it!"

The Martian grabbed the altar rail and vaulted over it, coming perilously close to the glowing reactor. He clawed at the towering, bearded Vorster.

Calmly the cultist reached out and slipped one long arm through the pinwheeling chaos of Weiner's threshing limbs. He touched his fingertips to the Martian's throat for a fraction of a second.

Weiner fell like a dead man.

three

"Are you all right now?" Kirby asked, dry-throated.

Weiner stirred. "Where's that girl?"

"The one with the surgery?"

"No," he rasped. "The esper. I want her near me again."

Kirby glanced at the slender, blue-haired girl. She nodded tensely and took Weiner's hand. The Martian's face was bright with sweat, and his eyes were still wild. He lay back, head propped on pillows, cheeks hollow.

They were in a sniffer palace across the street from the Vorster hall. Kirby had had to carry the Martian out of the place himself, slung across his shoulders; the Vorsters did not let robots in. The sniffer palace seemed as good a place as any to take him.

The esper girl had come over to them as Kirby staggered into the place. She was a Vorster, too—the blue hair was the tip-off—but apparently she had finished her worship for the day and was topping things off with a quick inhalation. With instant sympathy she had bent to peer at Weiner's flushed, sweat-flecked face. She had asked Kirby if his friend had had a stroke.

"I'm not sure what happened to him," Kirby said. "He was drunk and began to make trouble in the Vorster place. The leader of the service touched his throat."

The girl smiled. She was waif-like, fragile, no more than eighteen or nineteen. Cursed with talent. She closed her eyes, took Weiner's hand, clutched the thick wrist until the

Martian revived. Kirby did not know what she had done. All this was mystery to him.

Now, strength flowing back into him visibly from moment to moment, Weiner tried to sit up. He seized the girl's hand and held it. She did not attempt to break free.

He said, "What did they hit me with?"

"It was a momentary alteration of your charge," the girl told him. "He turned off your heart and brain for a thousandth of a second. There will be no permanent damage."

"How'd he do it? He just touched me with his fingers."

"There is a technique. But you'll be all right."

Weiner eyed the girl. "You an esper? You reading my mind right now?"

"I'm an esper, but I don't read minds. I'm just an empath. You're all churned up with hatred. Why don't you go back across the street? Ask him to forgive you. I know he will. Let him teach you. Have you read Vorst's book?"

"Why don't you just go to hell?" Weiner said casually. "No, don't. You're too cute. We got some cute espers on Mars, too. You want some fun tonight? My name's Nat Weiner, and this is my friend, Ron Kirby. *Reynolds* Kirby. He's a stuffed shirt, but we can give him the slip." The Martian's grip on the slender arm grew tighter. "What do you say?"

The girl didn't say anything. She simply frowned, and Weiner made a strange face and released her arm. Kirby, watching, had to repress a grin. Weiner was running into trouble all over the place. This was a complicated world.

"Go across the street," the girl whispered. "They'll help you there."

She turned without waiting for a reply and faded into the dimness. Weiner passed a hand over his forehead as though brushing cobwebs from his brain. He struggled to his feet, ignoring Kirby's proffered arm.

"What kind of place is this?" he asked.

"A sniffer palace."

"Will they preach to me here?"

"They'll just fog your brain a little," said Kirby. "Want to try?"

"Sure. I told you I wanted to try everything. I don't get a chance to come to Earth every day."

Weiner grinned, but it was a somber grin. He didn't seem to have the bounce he had had an hour ago. Of course, getting knocked out by the Vorster had sobered him some. He was still game, though, ready to soak up all the sins this wicked planet had to offer.

Kirby wondered whether he was making as big a mess of this assignment as it seemed. There was no way of knowing—not yet. Later, of course, Weiner might well protest the handling he had received, and Kirby might find himself abruptly transferred to less sensitive duties. That was not a pleasant thought. He regarded his career as an important matter, perhaps the only important matter in his life. He did not want to wreck it in a night.

They moved toward the sniffer booths.

"Tell me," Weiner said. "Do those people really believe all that crap about the electron?"

"I really don't know. I haven't made a study of it, Nat."

"You've watched the movement appear. How many members does it have now?"

"A couple of million, I guess."

"That's plenty. We have only seven million people on all of Mars. If you've got this many joining this nutty cult—"

"There are lots of new religious sects on Earth today," Kirby said. "It's an apocalyptic time. People are hungry for reassurance. They feel the Earth's being left behind by the stream of events. So they look for a unity, for some way out of all the confusion and fragmentation."

"Let them come to Mars if they want a unity. We got work for everybody, and no time to stew about the allness of it all." Weiner guffawed. "The hell with it. Tell me about this sniffer stuff."

"Opium's out of fashion. We inhale the more exotic mercaptans. The hallucinations are said to be entertaining."

"*Said* to be? Don't you know? Kirby, don't you have firsthand information about *anything*? You aren't even alive. You're just a zombi. A man needs some vices, Kirby."

The U.N. man thought of the Nothing Chamber waiting for him in the lofty tower on balmy Tortola. His face was a stony mask. He said, "Some of us are too busy for vices. But this visit of yours is likely to be a great education for me, Nat. Have a sniff."

A robot rolled up to them. Kirby clapped his right thumb against the lambent yellow plate set in the robot's chest. The light brightened as Kirby's print-pattern was recorded.

"We'll bill your Central," the robot said. Its voice was absurdly deep: pitch troubles on the master tape, Kirby suspected. When the metal creature rolled away, it was listing a bit to starboard. Rusty in the gut, he figured. An even chance that he wouldn't get billed. He picked up a sniffer mask and handed it to Weiner, who sprawled out comfortably on the couch along the wall of the booth. Weiner donned the mask. Kirby took another and slipped it over his nose and mouth. He closed his eyes and settled into the webfoam cradle near the booth's entrance. A moment passed; then he tasted the gas creeping into his nasal passages. It was a revolting sour-sweet smell, a sulfuric smell.

Kirby waited for the hallucination.

There were people who spent hours each day in these booths, he knew. The government kept raising the tax to discourage the sniffers, but they came anyway, even at ten, twenty, thirty dollars a sniff. The gas itself wasn't addictive, not in the metabolic way that heroin got to you. It was more of a psychological addiction, something you could break if you really tried, but which nobody cared to try to break: like the sex addiction, like mild alcoholism. For some it was a kind of religion. Everyone to his own creed; this was a crowded world, harboring many beliefs.

A girl made of diamonds and emeralds was walking through Kirby's brain.

The surgeons had cut away every scrap of living flesh on her body. Her eyeballs had the cold glitter of precious gems; her breasts were globes of white onyx tipped with ruby; her lips were slabs of alabaster; her hair was fashioned from strings of yellow gold. Blue fire flickered around her, Vorster fire, crackling strangely.

She said, "You're tired, Ron. You need to get away from yourself."

"I know. I'm using the Nothing Chamber every other day now. I'm fighting off a crackup."

"You're too rigid, that's your trouble. Why don't you visit my surgeon? Have yourself changed. Get rid of all that stupid meat. For this I say, that flesh and blood cannot inherit the kingdom of God; neither doth corruption inherit incorruption."

"No," Kirby muttered. "It isn't so. All I need is some rest. A good swim, sunshine, decent amount of sleep. But they dumped that mad Martian on me."

The hallucination laughed shrilly, rippled her arms, performed a sinuous convolution. They had sliced away fingers and replaced them with spikes of ivory. Her fingernails were of polished copper. The mischievous tongue that flicked out from between the alabaster lips was a serpent of gaudy flexiplast. "Behold," she crooned voluptuously, "I show you a mystery. We shall not all sleep, but we shall all be changed."

"In a moment," Kirby said. "In the twinkling of an eye. The trumpet shall sound."

"And the dead shall be raised incorruptible. Do it, Ron. You'll look so much handsomer. Maybe you can hold the next marriage together a little better, too. You miss her—admit it. You ought to see what she looks like now. Full fathom five thy loved one lies. But she's happy. For this corruptible must put on incorruption, and this mortal must put on immortality."

"I'm a human being," Kirby protested. "I'm not going

to turn myself into a walking museum piece like you. Or like *her*, for that matter. Even if it's becoming fashionable for men to have it done."

The blue glow began to pulse and throb around the vision in his brain. "You need something, though, Ron. The Nothing Chamber isn't the answer. It's—nothing. Affiliate yourself. Belong. Work isn't the answer, either. Join. Join. You won't carve yourself? All right, become a Vorster, then. Surrender to the Oneness. Let death be swallowed up in victory."

"Can't I just remain myself?" Kirby cried.

"What you are isn't enough. Not now. Not any more. These are hard times. A troubled world. The Martians make fun of us. The Venusians despise us. We need new organization, new strength. The sting of death is in sin, and the strength of sin is the law. Grave, where is thy victory?"

A riotous swirl of colors danced through Kirby's mind. The surgically altered woman pirouetted, leaped and bobbed, flaunted the jewel-bedecked flamboyance of herself in his face. Kirby quivered. He clawed fitfully at the mask. For this nightmare he had paid good money? How could people let themselves become addicts of this sort of thing—this tour through the swamps of one's own mind?

Kirby wrenched the sniffer mask away and threw it to the floor of the booth. He sucked clean air into his lungs, fluttered his eyes, returned to reality.

He was alone in the booth.

The Martian, Weiner, was gone.

four

The robot who ran the sniffer palace was of no help.

"Where'd he go?" Kirby demanded.

"He left," came the rusty reply. "Eighteen dollars sixty cents. We will bill your Central."

"Did he say where he was going?"

"We did not converse. He left. *Awwwrk!* We did not converse. I will bill your Central. *Awwwrk!*"

Sputtering a curse, Kirby rushed out into the street. He glanced involuntarily at the sky. Against the darkness he saw the lemon-colored letters of the timeglow streaming in the firmament, irregularly splotched with red:

2205 HOURS EASTERN STANDARD TIME
WEDNESDAY MAY 8 2077
BUY FREEBLES—THEY CRUNCH!

Two hours to midnight. Plenty of time for that lunatic colonial to get himself in trouble. The last thing Kirby wanted was to have a drunken, perhaps hallucinated Weiner rampaging around in New York. This assignment hadn't entirely been one of rendering hospitality. Part of Kirby's job was to keep an eye on Weiner. Martians had come to Earth before. The libertarian society was a heady wine for them.

Where had he gone?

One place to look was the Vorster hall. Maybe Weiner had gone back to raise some more hell over there. With sweat bursting from every pore, Kirby sprinted across the street, dodging the rocketing teardrops as they turbined past, and rushed into the shabby cultist chapel. The service was still going on. It didn't seem as though Weiner were there, though. Everyone obediently knelt in his pew, and there were no shouts, no screams of boozy laughter. Kirby silently loped down the aisle, checking every bench. No Weiner. The girl with the surgical face was still there, and she smiled and stretched a hand toward him. For one bizarre moment Kirby was catapulted back into his sniffer hallucination, and his flesh crawled. Then he recovered himself. He managed a faint smile to be polite and got out of the Vorster place as fast as he could.

He caught the slidewalk and let it carry him three blocks in a random direction. No Weiner. Kirby got off and found himself in front of a public Nothing Chamber place, where for twenty bucks an hour you could get wafted off to luscious oblivion. Perhaps Weiner had wandered in there, eager to try every mind-sapping diversion the city had to offer. Kirby went in.

Robots weren't in charge here. A genuine flesh-and-blood entrepreneur came forward, a four-hundred-pounder, opulent with chins. Small eyes buried in fat regarded Kirby doubtfully.

"Want an hour of rest, friend?"

"I'm looking for a Martian," Kirby blurted. "About so high, big shoulders, sharp cheekbones."

"Haven't seen him."

"Look, maybe he's in one of your tanks. This is important. It's U.N. business."

"I don't care if it's the business of God Almighty. I haven't seen him." The fat man glanced only briefly at Kirby's identification plaque. "What do you want me to do—open my tanks for you? He didn't come in here."

"If he does, don't let him rent a chamber," Kirby begged. "Stall him and phone U.N. Security right away."

"I got to rent him if he wants. We run a public hall here, buddy. You want to get me in trouble? Look, you're all worked up. Why don't *you* climb into a tank for a little while? It'll do wonders for you. You'll feel like—"

Kirby wheeled and ran out. There was nausea in the pit of his stomach, perhaps induced by the hallucinogen. There was also fright and a goodly jolt of anger. He visualized Weiner clubbed in some dark alley, his stocky body expertly vivisected for the bootleg organ banks. A worthy fate, perhaps, but it would raise hob with Kirby's reliability rating. More likely was it that Weiner, bashing around like a Chinese bull—was that the right simile, Kirby wondered?—would stir up some kind of mess that would be blasphemously difficult to clean up.

Kirby had no idea where to look. A communibooth presented itself on the corner of the next street, and he jumped in, opaquing the screens. He rammed his identification plaque into the slot and punched for U.N. Security.

The cloudy little screen grew clear. The pudgy, bearded face of Lloyd Ridblom appeared.

"Night squad," Ridblom said. "Hello, Ron. Where's your Martian?"

"Lost him. He gave me the slip in a sniffer palace."

Ridblom became instantly animated. "Want me to slap a televector on him?"

"Not yet," Kirby said. "I'd rather he didn't know we were upset about his disappearance. Put the vector on me, instead, and keep contact. And open up a routine net for him. If he shows, notify me right away. I'll call back in an hour to change the instructions if nothing's happened by then."

"Maybe he's been kidnapped by Vorsters," Ridblom suggested. "They're draining his blood for altar wine."

"Go to hell," Kirby said. He stepped out of the booth and put his thumbs briefly to his eyeballs. Slowly, purposelessly, he strolled toward the slidewalk and let it take him back to the Vorster hall. A few people were coming out of it now. There was the girl with the iridescent earshells; she wasn't content to haunt his hallucinations—she had to keep intersecting his path in real life, too.

"Hello," she said. Her voice was gentle, at least. "I'm Vanna Marshak. Where'd your friend go?"

"I'm wondering that myself. He vanished a little while ago."

"Are you supposed to be in charge of him?"

"I'm supposed to be watching him, anyhow. He's a Martian, you know."

"I didn't. He's certainly hostile to the Brotherhood, isn't he? That was sad, the way he erupted during the service. He must be terribly ill."

"Terribly drunk," Kirby said. "It happens to all the Martians who come here. The iron bars are lifted for them, and they think anything goes. Can I buy you a drink?" he added mechanically.

"I don't drink, thanks. But I'll accompany you if you want one."

"I don't *want* one. I *need* one."

"You haven't told me your name."

"Ron Kirby. I'm with the U.N. I'm a minor bureaucrat. No, I'll correct that: a major bureaucrat who gets paid like a minor one. We can go in here."

He nudged the doorstud of a bar on the corner. The sphincter whickered open and admitted them. She smiled warmly. She was about thirty, Kirby guessed. Not easy to tell, with all that hardware where her face used to be.

"Filtered rum," he said.

Vanna Marshak leaned close to him. She wore some subtle and unfamiliar perfume. "Why did you bring him to the Brotherhood house?" she asked.

He downed his drink as though it were fruit juice. "He wanted to see what the Vorsters were like. So I took him."

"I take it you're unsympathetic personally?"

"I don't have any real opinion. I've been too busy to pay much attention."

"That's not true," she said easily. "You think it's a nut-cult, don't you?"

Kirby ordered a second drink. "All right," he admitted. "I do. It's a shallow opinion based on no real information at all."

"You haven't read Vorst's book?"

"No."

"If I give you a copy, will you read it?"

"Imagine," he said. "A proselyte with a heart of gold." He laughed. He was feeling drunk again.

"That isn't really very funny," she said. "You're hostile to surgical alterations, too, aren't you?"

"My wife had a complete face job done. While she was still my wife. I got so angry about it that she left me. Three years ago. She's dead now. She and her lover went down in a rocket crash off New Zealand."

"I'm terribly sorry," Vanna Marshak said. "But I wouldn't have had this done to myself if I had known about Vorst then. I was uncertain. Insecure. Today I know where I'm heading—but it's too late to have my real face back. It's rather attractive, I think, anyway."

"Lovely," Kirby said. "Tell me about Vorst."

"It's very simple. He wants to restore spiritual values in the world. He wants us all to become aware of our common nature and our higher goals."

"Which we can express by watching Cerenkov radiation in rundown lofts," Kirby said.

"The Blue Fire's just trimming. It's the inner message that counts. Vorst wants to see mankind go to the stars. He wants us to get out of our muddle and confusion and begin to mine our real talents. He wants to save the espers who are going insane every day, harness them, put them together to work for the next great step in human progress."

"I see," said Kirby gravely. "Which is?"

"I told you. Going to the stars. You think we can stop with Mars and Venus? There are millions of planets out there. Waiting for man to find a way to reach them. Vorst thinks he knows that way. But it calls for a union of mental energies, a blending, a—oh, I know this sounds mystical. But he's got something. And it heals the troubled soul, too. That's the short-range purpose: the communion, the binding-up of wounds. And the long-range goal is getting to the stars. Of course, we've got to overcome the frictions between the planets—get the Martians to be more tolerant, and then somehow reestablish contact with the people on Venus, if there's anything human still left in them—do you see that there are possibilities here, that it isn't mumbo jumbo and fraud?"

Kirby didn't see anything of the kind. It sounded hazy and incoherent to him. Vanna Marshak had a soft, persuasive voice, and there was an earnestness about her that made her appealing. He could even forgive her for what she had let the knife-wielders do to her face. But when it came to Vorst—

The communicator in his pocket bleeped. It was a signal from Ridblom, and it meant call the office right away. Kirby got to his feet.

"Excuse me a minute," he said. "Something important to tend to—"

He lurched across the barroom, caught himself, took a deep breath and got into the booth. Into the slot went the plaque; trembling fingers punched out the number.

Ridblom appeared on the screen again.

"We've found your boy," the pudgy Security man announced blandly.

"Dead or alive?"

"Alive, unfortunately. He's in Chicago. He stopped off at the Martian Consulate, borrowed a thousand dollars from the consul's wife, and tried to rape her in the bargain. She got rid of him and called the police, and they called me. We have a five-man tracer on him now. He's heading for a Vorster cell on Michigan Boulevard, and he's drunk as a lord. Should we intercept him?"

Kirby bit his lip in anguish. "No. No. He's got immunity, anyway. Let me handle this. Is there a chopper in the U.N. port I can borrow?"

"Sure. But it'll take you at least forty minutes to get to Chi, and—"

"That's plenty of time. Here's what I want you to do: get hold of the prettiest esper you can find in Chicago, maybe an empath, some sexy kid, Oriental if possible, something like that one who had the burnout in Kyoto last week. Plunk her down between Weiner and that Vorster place and turn her loose on him. Have her charm him into submission. Have her stall him in any way possible until I can get there, and if she has to part with her honor in the process, tell her we'll give her a good price for it. If you can't find an esper, get hold of a persuasive policewoman, or something."

"I don't see why this is really necessary," Ridblom said. "The Vorsters can look out for themselves. I understand they've got some mysterious way of knocking a trouble-maker out so that he doesn't——"

"I know, Lloyd. But Weiner's already been knocked out once this evening. For all I know, a second jolt of the same stuff tonight might kill him. That would be very awkward all around. Just head him off."

Ridblom shrugged. "Thy will be done."

Kirby left the booth. He was cold sober again. Vanna Marshak was sitting at the bar where he had left her. At this distance and in this light there was something almost pretty about her artificial disfigurements.

She smiled. "Well?"

"They found him. He got to Chicago somehow, and he's about to raise some hell in the Vorster chapel there. I've got to go and lasso him."

"Be gentle with him, Ron. He's a troubled man. He needs help."

"Don't we all?" Kirby blinked suddenly. The thought of making the trip to Chicago alone struck him abruptly as being nasty. "Vanna?" he asked.

"Yes?"

"Are you going to be busy for the next couple of hours?"

five

The copter hovered over Chicago's sparkling gaiety. Below, Kirby saw the bright sheen of Lake Michigan, and the splendid mile-high towers that lined the lake. Above him blazed the local timeglow in chartreuse banded with deep blue:

2331 HOURS CENTRAL STANDARD TIME
WEDNESDAY MAY 8 2077
OGLEBAY REALTY—THE FINEST!

"Put her down," Kirby ordered.

The robopilot steered the copter toward a landing. It was impossible, of course, to risk the fierce wind currents in those deep canyons; they would have to land at a rooftop heliport. The landing was smooth. Kirby and Vanna rushed out. She had given him the Vorster message all the way from Manhattan, and at this point Kirby wasn't sure whether the cult was complete nonsense or some sinister conspiracy against the general welfare or a truly profound, spiritually uplifting creed or perhaps a bit of all three.

He thought he had the general idea. Vorst had cobbled together an eclectic religion, borrowing the confessional from Catholicism, absorbing some of the atheism of ur-Buddhism, adding a dose of Hindu reincarnation, and larding everything over with ultramodernistic trappings, nuclear reactors at every altar, and plenty of gabble about the holy electron. But there was also talk of harnessing the minds of espers to power a stardrive, of a communion even of non-esper minds, and—most startling of all, the big selling-point—personal immortality, not reincarnation, not the hope of Nirvana, but eternal life in the here-and-now present flesh. In view of Earth's population problems, immortality was low on any sane man's priority list. Immortality for other people, anyway; one was always willing to consider the extension of one's own life, wasn't one? Vorst preached the eternal life of the body, and the people were buying. In eight years the cult had gone from one cell to a thousand, from fifty followers to millions. The old religions were bankrupt. Vorst was handing out shining gold pieces, and if they were only fool's gold, it would take a while for the faithful to find that out.

"Come on," Kirby said. "There isn't much time."

He scrambled down the exit ramp, turning to take Vanna Marshak's hand and help her the last few steps. They hurried across the rooftop landing area to the gravshaft, stepped in, dropped to ground level in a dizzying five-second plunge. Local police were waiting in the street. They had three teardrops.

"He's a block from the Vorster place, Freeman Kirby," one of the policeman said. "The esper's been dragging him around for half an hour, but he's dead set on going there."

"What does he want there?" Kirby asked.

"He wants the reactor. He says he's going to take it back to Mars and put it to some worthwhile use."

Vanna gasped at the blasphemy. Kirby shrugged, sat back, watched the streets flashing by. The teardrop halted. Kirby saw the Martian across the street.

The girl who was with him was sultry, full-bodied, lush-looking. She had one arm thrust through his, and she was close to Weiner's side, cooing in his ear. Weiner laughed harshly and turned to her, pulled her close, then pushed her away. She clutched at him again. It was quite a scene, Kirby thought. The street had been cleared. Local police and a couple of Ridblom's men were watching grimly from the sidelines.

Kirby went forward and gestured to the girl. She sensed

instantly who he was, withdrew her arm from Weiner, and stepped away. The Martian swung around.

"Found me, did you?"

"I didn't want you to do anything you'd regret later on."

"Very loyal of you, Kirby. Well, as long as you're here, you can be my accomplice. I'm on my way to the Vorster place. They're wasting good fissionables in those reactors. You distract the priest, and I'm going to grab the blue blinker, and we'll all live happily ever after. Just don't let him shock you. That isn't fun."

"Nat—"

"Are you with me or aren't you, pal?" Weiner pointed toward the chapel, diagonally across the street a block away, in a building almost as shabby as the one in Manhattan. He started toward it.

Kirby glanced uncertainly at Vanna. Then he crossed the street behind Weiner. He realized that the altered girl was following, too.

Just as Weiner reached the entrance to the Vorster place, Vanna dashed forward and cut in front of him.

"Wait," she said. "Don't go in there to make trouble."

"Get out of my way, you phony-faced bitch!"

"Please," she said softly. "You're a troubled man. You aren't in harmony with yourself, let alone with the world around you. Come inside with me, and let me show you how to pray. There's much for you to gain in there. If you'd only open your mind, open your heart—instead of standing there so smug in your hatred, in your drunken unwillingness to see—"

Weiner hit her.

It was a backhand slap across the face. Surgical alteration jobs are fragile, and they aren't meant to be slapped. Vanna fell to her knees, whimpering, and pressed her hands over her face. She still blocked the Martian's way. Weiner drew his foot back as though he were going to kick her, and that was when Reynolds Kirby forgot he was paid to be a diplomat.

Kirby strode forward, caught Weiner by the elbow,

swung him around. The Martian was off balance. He clawed at Kirby for support. Kirby struck his hand down, brought a fist up, landed it solidly in Weiner's muscular belly. Weiner made a small oofing sound and began to rock backward. Kirby had not struck a human being in anger in thirty years, and he did not realize until that moment what a savage pleasure there could be in something so primordial. Adrenalin flooded his body. He hit Weiner again, just below the heart. The Martian, looking very surprised, sagged and went over backward, sprawling in the street.

"Get up," Kirby said, almost dizzy with rage.

Vanna plucked at his sleeve. "Don't hit him again," she murmured. Her metallic lips looked crumpled. Her cheeks glistened with tears. "Please don't hit him any more."

Weiner remained where he was, shaking his head vaguely. A new figure came forward: a small leathery-faced man, in late middle age. The Martian consul. Kirby felt his belly churn with apprehension.

The consul said, "I'm terribly sorry, Freeman Kirby. He's really been running amok, hasn't he? Well, we'll take jurisdiction now. What he needs is to have some of his own people tell him what a fool he's been."

Kirby stammered, "It was my fault. I lost sight of him. He shouldn't be blamed. He—"

"We understand perfectly, Freeman Kirby." The consul smiled benignly, gestured, nodded as three aides came forward and gathered the fallen Weiner into their arms.

Very suddenly the street was empty. Kirby stood, drained and stupefied, in front of the Vorster chapel, and Vanna was with him, and all the others were gone, Weiner vanishing like an ogre in a bad dream. It had not, Kirby thought, been a very successful evening. But now it was over.

Home, now.

An hour and a half would see him in Tortola. A quick, lonely swim in the warm ocean—then half an hour in the Nothing Chamber tomorrow. No, an hour, Kirby decided. It would take that much to undo this night's damage. An hour of disassociation, an hour of drifting on the amniotic tide, sheltered, warm, unbothered by the pressures of the world, an hour of blissful if cowardly escape. Fine. Wonderful.

Vanna said, "Will you come in now?"

"Into the chapel?"

"Yes. Please."

"It's late. I'll get you back to New York right away. We'll pay for any repairs that—that your face will need. The copter's waiting."

"Let it wait," Vanna said. "Come inside."

"I want to get home."

"Home can wait, too. Give me two hours with you, Ron. Just sit and listen to what they have to say in there. Come to the altar with me. You don't have to do anything but listen. It'll relax you, I promise that."

Kirby stared at her distorted, artificial face. Beneath the grotesque eyelids were real eyes—shining, imploring. Why was she so eager? Did they pay a finder's fee of salvation for every lost soul dragged into the Blue Fire? Or could it be, Kirby wondered, that she really and truly believed, that her heart and soul were bound up in this movement, that she was sincere in her conviction that the followers of Vorst would live through eternity, would live to see men ride to the distant stars?

He was so very tired.

He wondered how the security officers of the Secretariat would regard it if a high official like himself began to dabble in Vorsterism.

He wondered, too, if he had any career at all left to salvage, after tonight's fiasco with the Martian. What was there to lose? He could rest for a while. His head was splitting. Perhaps some esper in there would massage his frontal lobes for a while. Espers tended to be drawn to the Vorster chapels, didn't they?

The place seemed to have a pull. He had made his job his religion, but was that really good enough now, he asked himself? Perhaps it was time to unbend, time to shed the mask of aloofness, time to find out what it was that the multitudes were buying so eagerly in these chapels. Or perhaps it was just time to give in and let himself be pulled under by the tide of the new creed.

The sign over the door said:

BROTHERHOOD OF THE IMMANENT RADIANCE
COME YE ALL
YE WHO MAY NEVER DIE
HARMONIZE WITH THE ALL

"Will you?" Vanna said.

"All right," Kirby muttered. "I'm willing. Let's go harmonize with the All."

She took his hand. They stepped through the door. About a dozen people were kneeling in the pews. Up front the chapel leader was nudging the moderator rods out of the little reactor, and the first faint bluish glow was beginning to suffuse the room. Vanna guided Kirby into the last row. He looked toward the altar. The glow was deepening, casting a strange radiance on the plump, dogged-looking man at the front of the room. Now greenish-white, now purplish, now the Blue Fire of the Vorsters.

The opium of the masses, Kirby thought, and the hackneyed phrase sounded foolishly cynical as it echoed through his brain. What was the Nothing Chamber, after all, but the opium of the elite? And the sniffer palaces, what were they? At least here they went for the mind and soul, not for the body. It was worth an hour of his time to listen, at any rate.

"My brothers," said the man at the altar in a soft, fog-smooth voice, "we celebrate the underlying Oneness here. Man and woman, star and stone, tree and bird, all consist of atoms, and those atoms contain particles moving at wondrous speeds. They are the electrons, my brothers. They show us the way to peace, as I will make clear to you. They—"

Reynolds Kirby bowed his head. He could not bear to look at that glowing reactor, suddenly. There was a throbbing in his skull. He was distantly aware of Vanna beside him, smiling, warm, close.

I'm listening, Kirby thought. *Go on. Tell me! Tell me! I want to hear. God and the almighty electron help me—I want to hear!*

TWO

The Warriors of Light
2095

one

If Acolyte Third Level Christopher Mondschein had a weakness, it was that he wanted very badly to live forever. The yearning for everlasting life was a common enough human desire, and not really reprehensible. But Acolyte Mondschein carried it a little too far.

"After all," one of his superiors found it necessary to remind him, "your function in the Brotherhood is to look after the well-being of others. Not to feather your own nest, Acolyte Mondschein. Do I make that clear?"

"Perfectly clear, Brother," said Mondschein tautly. He felt ready to explode with shame, guilt, and anger. "I see my error. I ask forgiveness."

"It isn't a matter of forgiveness, Acolyte Mondschein," the older man replied. "It's a matter of understanding. I don't give a damn for forgiveness. What are your goals, Mondschein? What are you after?"

The acolyte hesitated a moment before answering— both because it was always good policy to weigh one's words before saying anything to a higher member of the Brotherhood, and because he knew he was on very thin ice. He tugged nervously at the pleats of his robe and let his eyes wander through the Gothic magnificence of the chapel.

They stood on the balcony, looking down at the nave. No service was in progress, but a few worshipers occupied the pews anyway, kneeling before the blue radiance of the small cobalt reactor on the front dais. It was the Nyack chapel of the Brotherhood of the Immanent Radiance,

47

third largest in the New York area, and Mondschein had joined it six months before, the day he turned twenty-two. He had hoped, at the time, that it was genuine religious feeling that had impelled him to pledge his fortunes to the Vorsters. Now he was not so sure.

He grasped the balcony rail and said in a low voice, "I want to help people, Brother. People in general and people in particular. I want to help them find the way. And I want mankind to realize its larger goals. As Vorst says—"

"Spare me the scriptures, Mondschein."

"I'm only trying to show you—"

"I know. Look, don't you understand that you've got to move upward in orderly stages? You can't go leapfrogging over your superiors, Mondschein, no matter how impatient you are to get to the top. Come into my office a moment."

"Yes, Brother Langholt. Whatever you say."

Mondschein followed the older man along the balcony and into the administrative wing of the chapel. The building was fairly new and strikingly handsome—a far cry from the shabby slum-area storefronts of the first Vorster chapels a quarter of a century before. Langholt touched a bony hand to the stud, and the door of his office irised quickly. They stepped through.

It was a small, austere room, dark and somber, its ceiling groined in good Gothic manner. Bookshelves lined the side walls. The desk was a polished ebony slab on which there glowed a miniature blue light, the Brotherhood's symbol. Mondschein saw something else on the desk: the letter he had written to District Supervisor Kirby, requesting a transfer to the Brotherhood's genetic center at Santa Fe.

Mondschein reddened. He reddened easily; his cheeks were plump and given to blushing. He was a man of slightly more than medium height, a little on the fleshy side, with dark coarse hair and close-set, earnest features. Mondschein felt absurdly immature by comparison with the gaunt, ascetic-looking man more than twice his age who was giving him this dressing-down.

Langholt said, "As you see, we've got your letter to Supervisor Kirby."

"Sir, that letter was confidential. I—"

"There are no confidential letters in this order, Mondschein! It happens that Supervisor Kirby turned this letter over to me himself. As you can see, he's added a memorandum."

Mondschein took the letter. A brief note had been scrawled across its upper left-hand corner: "He's awfully in a hurry, isn't he? Take him down a couple of pegs. R.K."

The acolyte put the letter down and waited for the withering blast of scorn. Instead, he found the older man smiling gently.

"Why did you want to go to Santa Fe, Mondschein?"

"To take part in the research there. And the—the breeding program."

"You're not an esper."

"Perhaps I've got latent genes, though. Or at least maybe some manipulation could be managed so my genes would be important to the pool. Sir, you've got to understand that I wasn't being purely selfish about this. I want to contribute to the larger effort."

"You can contribute, Mondschein, by doing your maintenance work, by prayer, by seeking converts. If it's in the cards for you to be called to Santa Fe, you'll be called in due time. Don't you think there are others much older than you who'd like to go there? Myself? Brother Ashton? Supervisor Kirby himself? You walk in off the street, so to speak, and after a few months you want a ticket to utopia. Sorry. You can't have one that easily, Acolyte Mondschein."

"What shall I do now?"

"Purify yourself. Rid yourself of pride and ambition. Get down and pray. Do your daily work. Don't look for rapid preferment. It's the best way *not* to get what you want."

"Perhaps if I applied for missionary service," Mondschein suggested. "To join the group going to Venus—"

Langholt sighed. "There you go again! Curb your ambition, Mondschein!"

"I meant it as a penance."

"Of course. You imagine that those missionaries are likely to become martyrs. You also imagine that if by some fluke you go to Venus and don't get skinned alive, you'll come back here as a man of great influence in the Brotherhood, who'll be sent to Santa Fe like a warrior going to Valhalla. Mondschein, Mondschein, you're so transparent! You're verging on heresy, Mondschein, when you refuse to accept your lot."

"Sir, I've never had any traffic with the heretics. I—"

"I'm not accusing you of anything," Langholt said heavily. "I'm simply warning you that you're heading in an unhealthy direction. I fear for you. Look—" He thrust the incriminating letter to Kirby into a disposal unit, where it flamed and was gone instantly. "I'll forget that this whole episode ever happened. But don't you forget it. Walk more humbly, Mondschein. Walk more humbly, I say. Now go and pray. Dismissed."

"Thank you, Brother," Mondschein muttered.

His knees felt a little shaky as he made his way from the room and took the spiral slideshaft downward into the chapel proper. All things considered, he knew he had got off lightly. There could have been a public reprimand. There could have been a transfer to some not very desirable place, like Patagonia or the Aleutians. They might even have separated him from the Brotherhood entirely.

It had been a massive mistake to go over Langholt's head, Mondschein agreed. But how could a man help it? To die a little every day, while in Santa Fe they were choosing the ones who would live forever—it was intolerable to be on the outside. Mondschein's spirit sank at the awareness that now he had almost certainly cut himself off from Santa Fe for good.

He slipped into a rear pew and stared solemnly toward the cobalt-60 cube on the altar.

Let the Blue Fire engulf me, he begged. *Let me rise purified and cleansed.*

Sometimes, kneeling before the altar, Mondschein had felt the ghostly flicker of a spiritual experience. That was the most he ever felt, for, though he was an acolyte of the Brotherhood of the Immanent Radiance, and was a second-generation member of the cult, at that, Mondschein was not a religious man. Let others have ecstasies before the altar, he thought. Mondschein knew the cult for what it was: a front operation masking an elaborate program of genetic research. Or so it seemed to him, though there were times when he had his doubts which was the front and which the underlying reality. So many others appeared to derive spiritual benefits from the Brotherhood—while he had no proof that the laboratories at Santa Fe were accomplishing anything at all.

He closed his eyes. His head sank forward on his breast. He visualized electrons spinning in their orbits. He silently repeated the Electromagnetic Litany, calling off the stations of the spectrum.

He thought of Christopher Mondschein living through the ages. A stab of yearning sliced into him while he was still telling off the middling frequencies. Long before he got to the softer X rays, he was in a sweat of frustration, sick with the fear of dying. Sixty, seventy more years and his number was up, while at Santa Fe—

Help me. Help me. Help me.

Somebody help me. I don't want to die!

Mondschein looked to the altar. The Blue Fire flickered as though to mock him by going out altogether. Oppressed by the Gothic gloom, Mondschein sprang to his feet and rushed out into the open air.

two

He was a conspicuous figure in his indigo robe and monkish hood. People stared at him as though he had some supernatural power. They did not look closely enough to see that he was only an acolyte, and, though many of them were Vorsters themselves, they never managed to understand that the Brotherhood had no truck with the supernatural. Mondschein did not have a high regard for the intelligence of laymen.

He stepped aboard the slidewalk. The city loomed around him, towers of travertine that took on a greasy cast in the dying reddish glow of a March afternoon. New York City had spread up the Hudson like a plague, and skyscrapers were marching across the Adirondacks; Nyack, here, had long since been engulfed by the metropolis. The air was cool. There was a smoky tang in it; probably a fire raging in a forest preserve, thought Mondschein darkly. He saw death on all sides.

His modest apartment was five blocks from the chapel. He lived alone. Acolytes needed a waiver to marry and were forbidden to have transient liaisons. Celibacy did not weigh heavily on Mondschein yet, though he had hoped to shed it when he was transferred to Santa Fe. There was talk of lovely, willing young female acolytes at Santa Fe. Surely not *all* the breeding experiments were done through artificial insemination, Mondschein hoped.

No matter now. He could forget Santa Fe. His impulsive letter to Supervisor Kirby had smashed everything.

Now he was trapped forever on the lower rungs of the

Vorster ladder. In due course they would take him into the Brotherhood, and he would wear a slightly different robe and grow a beard, perhaps, and preside over services, and minister to the needs of his congregation.

Fine. The Brotherhood was the fastest-growing religious movement on Earth, and surely it was a noble work to serve in the cause. But a man without a religious vocation would not be happy presiding over a chapel, and Mondschein had no calling at all. He had sought to fulfill his own ends by enrolling as an acolyte, and now he saw the error of that ambition.

He was caught. Just another Vorster Brother now. There were thousands of chapels all over the world. Membership in the Brotherhood was something like five hundred million today. Not bad in a single generation. The older religions were suffering. The Vorsters had something to offer that the others did not: the comforts of science, the assurance that beyond the spiritual ministry there was another that served the Oneness by probing into the deepest mysteries. A dollar contributed to your local Vorster chapel might help pay for the development of a method to assure immortality, personal immortality. That was the pitch, and it worked well. Oh, there were imitators, lesser cults, some of them rather successful in their small way. There was even a Vorster heresy now, the Harmonists, the peddlers of the Transcendent Harmony, an offshoot of the parent cult. Mondschein had chosen the Vorsters, and he had a lingering loyalty to them, for he had been raised as a worshiper of the Blue Fire. But—

"Sorry. Million pardons."

Someone jostled him on the slidewalk. Mondschein felt a hand slap against his back, dealing him a hard jolt that almost knocked him down. Staggering a bit, he recovered and saw a broad-shouldered man in a simple blue business tunic moving swiftly away. Clumsy idiot, Mondschein thought. There's room for everyone on the walk. What's his hellish hurry?

Mondschein adjusted his robes and his dignity. A soft voice said, "Don't go into your apartment, Mondschein.

Just keep moving. There's a quickboat waiting for you at the Tarrytown station."

No one was near him. "Who said that?" he demanded tensely.

"Please relax and cooperate. You aren't going to be harmed. This is for your benefit, Mondschein."

He looked around. The nearest person was an elderly woman, fifty feet behind him on the slidewalk, who quickly threw him a simpering smile as though asking for a blessing. Who had spoken? For one wild moment Mondschein thought that he had turned into a telepath, some latent power breaking through in a delayed maturity. But no, it had been a voice, not a thought-message. Mondschein understood. The stumbling man must have planted a two-way Ear on him with that slap on the back. A tiny metallic transponding plaque, perhaps half a dozen molecules thick, some miracle of improbable subminiaturization—Mondschein did not bother to search for it.

He said, "Who are you?"

"Never mind that. Just go to the station and you'll be met."

"I'm in my robes."

"We'll handle that, too," came the calm response.

Mondschein nibbled his lip. He was not supposed to leave the immediate vicinity of his chapel without permission from a superior, but there was no time for that now, and in any event he had no intention of bucking the bureaucracy so soon after his rebuke. He would take his chances.

The slidewalk sped him ahead.

Soon the Tarrytown station drew near. Mondschein's stomach roiled with tension. He could smell the acrid fumes of quickboat fuel. The chill wind cut through his robes, so that his shivering was not entirely from uneasiness. He stepped from the slidewalk and entered the station, a gleaming yellowish-green dome with lambent plastic walls. It was not particularly crowded. The commuters from downtown had not yet begun to arrive, and the outward-bound rush would come later in the day, at the dinner hour.

Figures approached him. The voice coming from the device on his back said, "Don't stare at them, but just follow behind them casually."

Mondschein obeyed. There were three of them, two men and a slim, angular-faced woman. They led him on a sauntering stroll past the chattering newsfax booth, past the bootblack stands, past the row of storage lockers. One of the men, short and square-headed, with thick, stubby yellow hair, slapped his palm against a locker to open it. He drew out a bulky package and tucked it under one arm. As he cut diagonally across the station toward the men's washroom, the voice said to Mondschein, "Wait thirty seconds and follow him."

The acolyte pretended to study the newsfax ticker. He did not feel enthusiastic about his present predicament, but he sensed that it would be useless and possibly harmful to resist. When the thirty seconds were up, he moved toward the washroom. The scanner decided that he was suitably male, and the ADMIT sign flashed. Mondschein entered.

"Third booth," the voice murmured.

The blond man was not in sight. Mondschein entered the booth and found the package from the locker propped against the seat. On an order, he picked it up and opened the clasps. The wrapper fell away. Mondschein found himself holding the green robe of a Harmonist Brother.

The heretics? What in the world—

"Put it on, Mondschein."

"I can't. If I'm seen in it—"

"You won't be. Put it on. We'll guard your own robe until you get back."

He felt like a puppet. He shrugged out of his robe, put it on a hook, and donned the unfamiliar uniform. It fitted well. There was something clipped to the inner surface: a thermoplastic mask, Mondschein realized. He was grateful for that. Unfolding it, he pressed it to his face and held it there until it took hold. The mask would disguise his features just enough so that he need not fear recognition.

Carefully Mondschein put his own robe within the wrapper and sealed it.

"Leave it on the seat," he was told.

"I don't dare. If it's lost, how will I ever explain?"

"It will not be lost, Mondschein. Hurry now. The quickboat's about to leave."

Unhappily, Mondschein stepped from the booth. He viewed himself in the mirror. His face, normally plump, now looked gross: bulging cheeks, stubbly jowls, moist and thickened lips. Unnatural dark circles rimmed his eyes as though he had caroused for a week. The green robe was strange, too. Wearing the outfit of heresy made him feel closer to his own organization than ever before.

The slim woman came forward as he emerged into the waiting room. Her cheekbones were like hatchet blades, and her eyelids had been surgically replaced by shutters of fine platinum foil. It was an outmoded fashion of the previous generation; Mondschein could remember his mother coming from the cosmetic surgeon's office with her face transformed into a grotesque mask. No one did that any more. This woman had to be at least forty, Mondschein thought, though she looked much younger.

"Eternal harmony, Brother," she said huskily.

Mondschein fumbled for the proper Harmonist response. Improvising, he said, "May the Oneness smile upon you."

"I'm grateful for your blessing. Your ticket's in order, Brother. Will you come with me?"

She was his guide, he realized. He had shed the Ear with his own robe. Queasily, he hoped he would get to see that garment again before long. He followed the slim woman to the loading platform. They might be taking him anywhere—Chicago, Honolulu, Montreal—

The quickboat sparkled in the floodlit station, graceful, elegant, its skin a burnished bluish-green. As they filed aboard, Mondschein asked the woman, "Where are we going?"

"Rome," she said.

three

Mondschein's eyes were wide as the monuments of antiquity flashed by. The Forum, the Colosseum, the Theater of Marcellus, the gaudy Victor Emmanuel Monument, the Mussolini Column—their route took them through the heart of the ancient city. He saw also the blue glow of a Vorster chapel as he whizzed down the Via dei Fori Imperiali, and that struck him as harshly incongruous here in this city of an older religion. The Brotherhood had a solid foothold here, though. When Gregory XVIII appeared in the window at his Vatican palace, he could still draw a crowd of hundreds of thousands of cheering Romans, but many of those same Romans would melt from the square after viewing the Pope and head for the nearest chapel of the Brotherhood.

Evidently the Harmonists were making headway here, too, Mondschein thought. But he kept his peace as the car sped northward out of the city.

"This is the Via Flaminia," his guide announced. "The old route was followed when the electronic roadbed was installed. They have a deep sense of tradition here."

"I'm sure they do," said Mondschein wearily. It was mid-evening by his time, and he had had nothing to eat but a snack aboard the quickboat. The ninety-minute journey had dumped him in Rome in the hours before dawn. A wintry mist hung over the city; spring was late. Mondschein's face itched fiercely beneath his mask. Fear chilled his fingers.

They halted in front of a drab brick building somewhere a few dozen miles north of Rome. Mondschein shivered as he hurried within. The woman with platinum eyelids led him up the stairs and into a warm, brightly lit room occupied by three men in green Harmonist robes. That confirmed it, Mondschein thought: *I'm in a den of heretics.*

They did not offer their names. One was short and squat, with a sallow face and bulbous nose. One was tall and spectrally thin, arms and legs like spider's limbs. The third was unremarkable, with pale skin and narrow, bland eyes. The squat one was the oldest and seemed to be in charge.

Without preamble he said, "So they turned you down, did they?"

"How—"

"Never mind how. We've been watching you, Mondschein. We hoped you'd make it. We want a man in Santa Fe just as much as you want to be there."

"Are you Harmonists?"

"Yes. What about some wine, Mondschein?"

The acolyte shrugged. The tall heretic gestured, and the slim woman, who had not left the room, came forward with a flask of golden wine. Mondschein accepted a glass, thinking dourly that it was almost certainly drugged. The wine was chilled and faintly sweet, like a middling-dry Graves. The others took wine with him.

"What do you want from me?" Mondschein asked.

"Your help," said the squat one. "There's a war going on, and we want you to join our side."

"I don't know of any wars."

"A war between darkness and light," said the tall heretic in a mild voice. "We are the warriors of light. Don't think we're fanatics, Mondschein. Actually, we're quite reasonable men."

"Perhaps you know," said the third of the Harmonists, "that our creed is derived from yours. We respect the teachings of Vorst, and we follow most of his ways. In fact, we regard ourselves as closer to the original teachings than the present hierarchy of the Brotherhood. We're a purifying body. Every religion needs its reformers."

Mondschein sipped his wine. He allowed his eyes to twinkle maliciously as he remarked, "Usually it takes a thousand years for the reformers to put in their appearance. This is only 2095. The Brotherhood's hardly thirty years old."

The squat heretic nodded. "The pace of our times is a fast one. It took the Christians three hundred years to get political control of Rome—from the time of Augustus to that of Constantine. The Vorsters didn't need that long. You know the story: there are Brotherhood men in every legislative body in the world. In some countries they've organized their own political parties. I don't need to tell you about the financial growth of the organization, either."

"And you purifiers urge a return to the old, simple ways of thirty years ago?" Mondschein asked. "The ramshackle buildings, the persecutions, and all the rest? Is that it?"

"Not really. We appreciate the uses of power. We simply feel that the movement's become sidetracked in irrelevancies. Power for its own sake has become more important than power for the sake of larger goals."

The tall one said, "The Vorster high command quibbles about political appointments and agitates for changes in the income tax structure. It's wasting time and energy fooling around with domestic affairs. Meanwhile the movement's drawn a total blank on Mars and Venus—not one chapel among the colonists, not even a start there, total rejection. And where are the great results of the esper breeding program? Where are the dramatic new leaps?"

"It's only the second generation," Mondschein said. "You have to be patient." He smiled at that—counseling patience to others—and added, "I think the Brotherhood is heading in the right direction."

"We don't, obviously," said the pale one. "When we failed to reform from within, we had to leave and begin our own campaign, parallel to the original one. The long-range goals are the same. Personal immortality through bodily regeneration. And full development of extrasensory powers, leading to new methods of communication and transportation. That's what we want—not the right to decide local tax issues."

Mondschein said, "First you get control of the governments. Then you concentrate on the long-range goals."

"Not necessary," snapped the squat Harmonist. "Direct action is what we're interested in. We're confident of success, too. One way or another, we'll achieve our purposes."

The slim woman gave Mondschein more wine. He tried to shake her away, but she insisted on filling his glass, and he drank. Then he said, "I presume you didn't waft me off to Rome just to tell me your opinion of the Brotherhood. What do you need me for?"

"Suppose we were to get you transferred to Santa Fe," the squat one said.

Mondschein sat bolt upright. His hand tightened on the wineglass, nearly breaking it.

"How could you do that?"

"Suppose we could. Would you be willing to obtain certain information from the laboratories there and transmit it to us?"

"Spy for you?"

"You could call it that."

"It sounds ugly," Mondschein said.

"You'd have a reward for it."

"It better be a good one."

The heretic leaned forward and said quietly, "We'll offer you a tenth-level post in our organization. You'd have to wait fifteen years to get that high in the Brotherhood. We're a much smaller operation; you can rise in our hierarchy much faster than where you are. An ambitious man like you could be very close to the top before he was fifty."

"But what good is it?" Mondschein asked. "To get close to the top in the second-best hierarchy?"

"Ah, but we won't be second-best! Not with the information you'll provide for us. That will allow us to grow. Millions of people will desert the Brotherhood for us when they see what we have to offer—all that *they* have, plus our own values. We'll expand rapidly. And you'll have a position of high rank, because you threw your lot in with us at the beginning."

Mondschein saw the logic of that. The Brotherhood was swollen already, wealthy, powerful, top-heavy with entrenched bureaucrats. There was no room for advancement there. But if he were to transfer his allegiance to a small but dynamic group with ambitions that rivaled his own—

"It won't work," he said sadly.

"Why?"

"Assuming you can wangle me into Santa Fe, I'll be screened by espers long before I get there. They'll know I'm coming as a spy, and they'll screen me out. My memories of this conversation will give me away."

The squat man smiled broadly. "Why do you think you'll remember this conversation? We have our espers, too, Acolyte Mondschein!"

four

―――――――――――――

The room in which Christopher Mondschein found himself was eerily empty. It was a perfect square, probably built within a tolerance of hundredths of a millimeter, and there was nothing at all in it but Mondschein himself. No furniture, no windows, not so much as a cobweb. Shifting his weight uncomfortably from foot to foot, he stared up at the high ceiling, searching without success for the source of the steady, even illumination. He did not even know what city he was in. They had taken him out of Rome just as the sun was rising, and he might be in Jakarta now, or Benares, or perhaps Akron.

He had profound misgivings about all this. The Harmonists had assured him that there would be no risks, but Mondschein was not so sure. The Brotherhood had not attained its eminence without developing ways of protecting itself. For all the assurances to the contrary, he might well be detected long before he got into those secret laboratories at Santa Fe, and it would not go happily for him afterward.

The Brotherhood had its way of punishing those who betrayed it. Behind the benevolence was a certain streak of necessary cruelty. Mondschein had heard the stories: the one about the regional supervisor in the Philippines who had let himself be beguiled into providing minutes of the high councils to certain anti-Vorsterite police officials, for example.

Perhaps it was apocryphal. Mondschein had heard that the man had been taken to Santa Fe to undergo the loss of his pain receptors. A pleasant fate, never to feel pain again? Hardly. Pain was the measure of safety. Without pain, how did one know whether something was too hot or too cold to touch? A thousand little injuries resulted: burns, cuts, abrasions. The body eroded away. A finger here, a nose there, an eyeball, a swatch of skin—why, someone could devour his own tongue and not realize it.

Mondschein shuddered. The seamless wall in front of him abruptly telescoped and a man entered the room. The wall closed behind him.

"Are you the esper?" Mondschein blurted nervously.

The man nodded. He was without unusual features. His face had a vaguely Eurasian cast, Mondschein imagined. His lips were thin, his hair glossily dark, his complexion almost olive. There was something of a fragile look to him.

"Lie down on the floor," the esper said in a soft, furry voice. "Please relax. You are afraid of me, and you should not be afraid."

"Why shouldn't I? You're going to meddle with my mind!"

"Please. Relax."

Mondschein gave it a try. He settled on the yielding, rubbery floor and put his hands by his sides. The esper sank into the lotus position in one corner of the room, not looking at Mondschein. The acolyte waited uncertainly.

He had seen a few espers before. There were a good many of them now; after years of doubt and confusion, their traits had been isolated and recognized more than a century ago, and a fair amount of deliberate esper-to-esper mating had increased their number. The talents were still unpredictable, though. Most of the espers had little control over their abilities. They were unstable individuals, besides, generally high-strung, often lapsing into psychosis under stress. Mondschein did not like the idea of being locked in a windowless room with a psychotic esper.

And what if the esper had a malicious streak? What if, instead of simply inducing selective amnesia in Mondschein, he decided to make wholesale alterations in his memory patterns? It might happen that—

"You can get up now," the esper said brusquely. "It's done."

"What's done?" Mondschein asked.

The esper laughed triumphantly. "You don't need to know, fool. It's done, that's all."

The wall opened a second time. The esper left. Mondschein stood up, feeling strangely empty, wondering somberly where he was and what was happening to him. He had been going home on the slidewalk, and a man had jostled him, and then—

A slim woman with improbable cheekbones and eyelids of glittering platinum foil said, "Come this way, please."

"Why should I?"

"Trust me. Come this way."

Mondschein sighed and let her lead him down a narrow corridor into another room, brightly painted and lit. A coffin-sized metal tank stood in one corner of the room. Mondschein recognized it, of course. It was a sensory deprivation chamber, a Nothing Chamber, in which one floated in a warm nutrient bath, sight and hearing cut off, gravity's pull negated. The Nothing Chamber was an instrument for total relaxation. It could also have more sinister uses: a man who spent too much time in a Nothing Chamber became pliant, easily indoctrinated.

"Strip and get in," the woman said.

"And if I don't?"

"You will."

"How long a setting?"

"Two and a half hours."

"Too long," Mondschein said. "Sorry. I don't feel that tense. Will you show me the way out of here?"

The woman beckoned. A robot rolled into the room, blunt-nosed, painted an ugly dull black. Mondschein had never wrestled with a robot, and he did not intend to try it now. The woman indicated the Nothing Chamber once more.

This is some sort of dream, Mondschein told himself. A very bad dream.

He began to strip. The Nothing Chamber hummed its readiness. Mondschein stepped into it and allowed it to engulf him. He could not see. He could not hear. A tube fed him air. Mondschein slipped into total passivity, into a fetal comfort. The bundle of ambitions, conflicts, dreams, guilts, lusts, and ideas that constituted the mind of Christopher Mondschein was temporarily dissolved.

In time, he woke. They took him from the Chamber— he was wobbly on his legs, and they had to steady him—and gave him his clothing. His robe, he noticed, was the wrong color: green, the heretic color. How had that happened? Was he being forcibly impressed into the Harmonist movement? He knew better than to ask questions. They were putting a thermoplastic mask on his face now. *I'm to travel incognito, it seems.*

In a short while Mondschein was at a quickboat station. He was appalled to see Arabic lettering on the signs. Cairo, he wondered? Algiers? Beirut? Mecca?

They had reserved a private compartment for him. The woman with the altered eyelids sat with him during the swift flight. Several times Mondschein attempted to ask questions, but she gave him no reply other than a shrug.

The quickboat landed at the Tarrytown station. Familiar territory at last. A timesign told Mondschein that this was Wednesday, March 13, 2095, 0705 hours Eastern Standard Time. It had been late Tuesday afternoon, he remembered distinctly, when he crept home in disgrace from the chapel after getting his comeuppance over the matter of a transfer to Santa Fe. Say, 1630 hours. Somewhere he had lost all of Tuesday night and a chunk of Wednesday morning, about fifteen hours in all.

As they entered the main waiting room, the slim woman at his side whispered, "Go into the washroom. Third booth. Change your clothes."

Greatly troubled, Mondschein obeyed. There was a package resting on the seat. He opened it and found that it contained his indigo acolyte's robe. Hurriedly he peeled off the green robe and donned his own. Remembering the face mask, he stripped that off, too, and flushed it away. He packed up the green robe and, not knowing what else to do with it, left it in the booth.

As he came out, a dark-haired man of middle years approached him, holding out his hand.

"Acolyte Mondschein!"

"Yes?" Mondschein said, not recognizing him, but taking the hand anyway.

"Did you sleep well?"

"I—yes," Mondschein said. "Very well." There was an exchange of glances, and suddenly Mondschein did not remember why he had gone into the washroom, nor what he had done in there, nor that he had worn a green robe and a thermoplastic mask on his flight from a country where Arabic was the main language, nor that he had been in any other country at all, nor, for that matter, that he had stepped bewildered from a Nothing Chamber not too many hours ago.

He now believed that he had spent a comfortable night at home, in his own modest dwelling. He was not sure what he was doing at the Tarrytown quickboat station at this hour of the morning, but that was only a minor mystery and not worth detailed exploration.

Finding himself unusually hungry, Mondschein bought a hearty breakfast at the food console on the lower level of the station. He bolted it briskly. By eight, he was at the Nyack chapel of the Brotherhood of the Immanent Radiance, ready to aid in the morning service.

Brother Langholt greeted him warmly. "Did yesterday's little talk upset you too much, Mondschein?"

"I'm settling down now."

"Good, good. You mustn't let your ambitions engulf you, Mondschein. Everything comes in due time. Will you check the gamma level on the reactor, please?"

"Certainly, Brother."

Mondschein stepped toward the altar. The Blue Fire seemed like a beacon of security in an uncertain world. The acolyte removed the gamma detector from its case and set about his morning tasks.

five

The message summoning him to Santa Fe arrived three weeks later. It landed on the Nyack chapel like a thunderbolt, striking down through layer after layer of authority before it finally reached the lowly acolyte.

One of Mondschein's fellow acolytes brought him the news, in an indirect way. "You're wanted in Brother Langholt's office, Chris. Supervisor Kirby's there."

Mondschein felt alarm. "What is it? I haven't done anything wrong—not that I know of, anyway."

"I don't think you're in trouble. It's something big, Chris. They're all shaken up. It's some kind of order out of Santa Fe." Mondschein received a curious stare. "What I think they said was that you're being shipped out there on a transfer."

"Very funny," Mondschein said.

He hurried to Langholt's office. Supervisor Kirby stood against the bookshelf on the left. He was a man enough like Langholt to be his brother. Both were tall, lean men in early middle age, with an ascetic look about them.

Mondschein had never seen the Supervisor at such close range before. The story was that Kirby had been a U.N. man, pretty high in the international bureaucracy, until his conversion fifteen or twenty years ago. Now he was a key man in the hierarchy, possibly one of the dozen most important in the entire organization. His hair was clipped short, and his eyes were an odd shade of green. Mondschein had difficulty meeting those eyes. Facing Kirby in the flesh, he wondered how he had ever found the nerve to write that letter to him, requesting a transfer to the Santa Fe labs.

Kirby smiled faintly. "Mondschein?"

"Yes, sir."

"Call me Brother, Mondschein. Brother Langholt here has said some good things about you."

He has? Mondschein thought in surprise.

Langholt said, "I've told the Supervisor that you're ambitious, eager, and enthusiastic. I've also pointed out that you've got those qualities to an excessive degree, in some ways. Perhaps you'll learn some moderation at Santa Fe."

Stunned, Mondschein said, "Brother Langholt, I thought my application for a transfer had been turned down."

Kirby nodded. "It's been opened again. We need some control subjects, you see. Non-espers. A few dozen acolytes have been requisitioned, and the computer tossed your name up. You fit the needs. I take it you still want to go to Santa Fe?"

"Of course, sir—Brother Kirby."

"Good. You'll have a week to wrap up your affairs here." The green eyes were suddenly piercing. "I hope you'll prove useful out there, Brother Mondschein."

Mondschein could not make up his mind whether he was being sent to Santa Fe as a belated yielding to his request or to get rid of him at Nyack. It seemed incomprehensible to him that Langholt would approve the transfer after having rejected it so scathingly a few weeks before. But the Vorster high ones moved in mysterious ways, Mondschein decided. He accepted the puzzling decision in good grace, asking no questions. When his week was up, he knelt in the Nyack chapel one last time, said good-bye to Brother Langholt, and went to the quickboat station for the noon flight westward.

He was in Santa Fe by mid-morning local time. The station there, he noticed, was thronged with blue-robed ones, more than he had ever seen in a public place at any one time. Mondschein waited at the station, uneasily eying the immensity of the New Mexican landscape. The sky was a strangely bright shade of blue, and visibility seemed unlimited. Miles away Mondschein saw bare sandstone mountains rising. A tawny desert dotted with grayish-green sagebrush surrounded the station. Mondschein had never seen so much open space before.

"Brother Mondschein?" a pudgy acolyte asked.

"That's right."

"I'm Brother Capodimonte. I'm your escort. Got your luggage? Good. Let's go, then."

A teardrop was parked in back. Capodimonte took Mondschein's lone suitcase and racked it. He was about forty, Mondschein guessed. A little old to be an acolyte. A roll of fat bulged over his collar at the back of his neck.

They entered the teardrop. Capodimonte activated it and it shot away.

"First time here?" he asked.

"Yes," Mondschein said. "I'm impressed by the countryside."

"It's marvelous stuff, isn't it? Life-enhancing. You get a sense of space here. And of history. Prehistoric ruins scattered all over the place. After you're settled, perhaps we can go up to Frijoles Canyon for a look at the cave dwellings. Does that kind of thing interest you, Mondschein?"

"I don't know much about it," he admitted. "But I'll be glad to look, anyway."

"What's your specialty?"

"Nucleonics," Mondschein said. "I'm a furnace tender."

"I was an anthropologist until I joined the Brotherhood. I spend my spare time out at the pueblos. It's good to step back into the past occasionally. Especially out here, when you see the future erupting with such speed all around you."

"They're really making progress, are they?"

Capodimonte nodded. "Coming along quite well, they tell me. Of course, I'm not an insider. Insiders don't get to leave the center much. But from what I hear, they're accomplishing great things. Look out there, Brother—that's the city of Santa Fe we're passing right now."

Mondschein looked. *Quaint* was the word that occurred to him. The city was small, both in area and in the size of its buildings, which seemed to be no higher than three or four stories anywhere. Even at this distance Mondschein could make out the dusky reddish-brown of adobe.

"I expected it to be much bigger," Mondschein said.

"Zoning. Historical monument and all that. They've kept it pretty well as it was a hundred years ago. No new construction's allowed."

Mondschein frowned. "What about the laboratory center, though?"

"Oh, that's not really in Santa Fe. Santa Fe's just the nearest big city. We're actually about forty miles north," said Capodimonte. "Up near the Picuris country. Still plenty of Indians there, you know."

They were beginning to climb now. The teardrop surged up hillside roads, and the vegetation began to change, the twisted, gnarled junipers and piñon pines giving way to dark stands of Douglas fir and ponderosas. Mondschein still found it hard to believe that he was soon to arrive at the genetic center. *It goes to show,* he told himself. The only way to get anywhere in the world was to stand up and yell.

He had yelled. They had scolded him for it—but they had sent him to Santa Fe anyhow.

To live forever! To surrender his body to the experimenters who were learning how to replace cell with cell, how to regenerate organs, how to restore youth. Mondschein knew what they were working on here. Of course, there were risks, but what of that? At the very worst, he'd die—but in the ordinary scheme of events that would happen anyway. On the other hand, he might be one of the chosen, one of the elect.

A gate loomed before them. Sunlight gleamed furiously from the metal shield.

"We're here," Capodimonte announced.

The gate began to open.

Mondschein said, "Won't I be given some kind of esper scanning before they let me in?"

Capodimonte laughed. "Brother Mondschein, you've

been getting a scanning for the last fifteen minutes. If there were any reason to turn you back, that gate wouldn't be opening now. Relax. And welcome. You've made it."

six

━━━━━━━━━━━━━━━━━━━━━━━━━━━━━━

The official name of the place was the Noel Vorst
Center for the Biological Sciences. It sprawled over some
fifteen square miles of plateau country, every last inch of
it ringed by a well-bugged fence. Within were dozens of
buildings—dormitories, laboratories, other structures of
less obvious purpose. The entire enterprise was under-
written by the contributions of the faithful, who gave
according to their means—a dollar here, a thousand
dollars there.

The center was heart and core of the Vorster operation.
Here the research was carried out that served to improve
the lives of Vorsters everywhere. The essence of the
Brotherhood's appeal was that it offered not merely
spiritual counseling—which the old religions could
provide just as well—but also the most advanced scientific
benefits. Vorster hospitals existed now in every major
population center. Vorster medics were at the forefront of
their profession. The Brotherhood of the Immanent Radiance healed both body and soul.

And, as the Brotherhood did not attempt to conceal,
the greater goal of the organization was the conquest of
death. Not merely the overthrow of disease, but the
downfall of age itself. Even before the Vorster movement
had begun, men had been making great progress in that
direction. The mean life expectancy was up to ninety-odd,
above one hundred in some countries. That was why the
Earth teemed with people, despite the stringent birth-
control regulations that were in effect almost everywhere.

Close to eleven billion people now, and the birth rate, though dropping sharply, was still greater than the death rate.

The Vorsters hoped to push the life expectancy still higher for those who wanted longer lives. A hundred and twenty, a hundred and fifty years—that was the immediate goal. Why not two hundred, three hundred, a thousand later on? "Give us everlasting life," the multitudes cried, and flocked to the chapels to make sure they were among the elect.

Of course, that prolongation of life would make the population problem all the more complex. The Brotherhood was aware of that. It had other goals designed to alleviate that problem. To open the galaxy to man—that was the real aim.

The colonization of the universe by humankind had already begun several generations before Noel Vorst founded his movement. Mars and Venus both had been settled, in differing ways. Neither planet had been hospitable to man, to begin with, so Mars had been changed to accommodate man, and man had been changed to survive on Venus. Both colonies were thriving now. Yet little had been accomplished toward solving the population crisis; ships would have to leave Earth day and night for hundreds of years in order to transport enough people to the colonies to make a dent in the multitudes on the home world, and that was economically impossible.

But if the extrasolar worlds could be reached, and if they did not need to be expensively Terraformed before they could be occupied, and if some new and reasonably economical means of transportation could be devised—

"That's a lot of ifs," Mondschein said.

Capodimonte nodded. "I don't deny that. But that's no reason not to try."

"You seriously think that there'll be a way to shoot people off to the stars on esper power?" Mondschein asked. "You don't think that that's a wild and fantastic dream?"

Smiling, Capodimonte said, "Wild and fantastic dreams keep men moving around. Chasing Prester John, chasing the Northwest Passage, chasing unicorns—well, this is our unicorn, Mondschein. Why all the skepticism? Look about you. Don't you see what's going on?"

Mondschein had been at the research center for a week. He still did not know his way around the place with any degree of confidence, but he had learned a great deal. He knew, for example, that an entire town of espers had been built on the far side of the dry wash that cut the center in half. Six thousand people lived there, none of them older than forty, all of them breeding like rabbits. Fertility Row, they called the place. It had special government dispensation for unlimited childbearing. Some of the families had five or six children.

That was the slow way of evolving a new kind of man. Take a bunch of people with unusual talents, throw them into a closed environment, let them pick their own mates and multiply the genetic pool—well, that was one way. Another was to work directly on the germ plasm. They were doing that here, too, in a variety of ways. Tecto-genetic microsurgery, polynuclear molding, DNA manipulation—they were trying everything. Cut and carve the genes, push the chromosomes around, get the tiny replicators to produce something slightly different from what had gone before—that was the aim.

How well was it working? That was hard to tell, so far. It would take five or six generations to evaluate the results. Mondschein, as a mere acolyte, did not have the equipment to judge for himself. Neither did most of those he had contact with—technicians, mainly. But they could speculate, and they did, far into the night.

What interested Mondschein, far more than the experiments in esper genetics, was the work on life span prolongation. Here, too, the Vorsters were building on an established body of technique. The organ banks provided replacements for most forms of bodily tissue; lungs, eyes, hearts, intestines, pancreases, kidneys, all could be implanted now, using the irradiation techniques to destroy the graft-rejecting immune reaction. But such piecemeal rejuvenation was not true immortality. The Vorsters sought a way to make the cells of the body regenerate lost tissue, so that the impulse toward continued life came from within, not through external grafts.

Mondschein did his bit. Like most of the bottom-grade people at the center, he was required to surrender a morsel of flesh every few days as experimental material. The biopsies were a nuisance, but they were part of the routine. He was a regular contributor to the sperm bank, too. As a non-esper, he was a good control subject for the work going on. How did you find the gene for teleportation? For telepathy? For any of the paranormal phenomena that were lumped under the blanket term of "esp"?

Mondschein cooperated. He played his humble part in the great campaign, aware that he was no more than an infantryman in the struggle. He went from laboratory to laboratory, submitting to tests and needles, and when he was not taking part in such enterprises, he carried out his own specialty, which was to serve as a maintenance man on the nuclear power plant that ran the entire center.

It was quite a different life from that in the Nyack chapel. No members of the public came here—no worshipers—and it was easy to forget that he was part of a religious movement. They held services here regularly, of course, but there was a professionalism about the worship that made it all seem rather perfunctory. Without some laymen in the house, it was hard to remain really dedicated to the cult of the Blue Fire.

In this more rarefied climate, Mondschein felt some of his seething impatience ebb away. Now he no longer could dream of going to Santa Fe, for he was there, on the spot, part of the experiments. Now he could only wait, and tick off the moments of progress, and hope.

He made new friends. He developed new interests. He went with Capodimonte to see the ancient ruins, and he went hunting in the Picuris Range with a lanky acolyte named Weber, and he joined the choral society and sang a lusty tenor.

He was happy here.

He did not know, of course, that he was here as a spy for heretics. All that had been deftly erased from his memory. In its place had been left a triggering mechanism, which went off one night in early September, and abruptly Mondschein felt a strange compulsion take hold.

It was the night of the Meson Sacrament, a feast that heralded the autumn solstice. Mondschein, wearing his blue robe, stood between Capodimonte and Weber in the chapel, watching the reactor glare on the altar, listening to the voice intoning, *"The world turns and the configurations change. There is a quantum jump in the lives of men, when doubts and fears are left behind and certainty is born. There is a flash as of light—a surge of inward radiation, a sense of Oneness with—"*

Mondschein stiffened. They were Vorst's words, words he had heard an infinity of times, so familiar to him that they had cut grooves in his brain. Yet now he seemed to be hearing them for the first time. When the words *"a sense of Oneness"* were pronounced, Mondschein gasped, gripped the seat in front of him, nearly doubled up in agony. He felt a sensation as of a blazing knife twisting in his bowels.

"Are you all right?" Capodimonte whispered.

Mondschein nodded. "Just—cramps—"

He forced himself to straighten up. But he was not all right, he knew. Something was wrong, and he did not know what. He was possessed. He was no longer his own master. Willy-nilly, he would obey an inner command whose nature he did not at the moment know, but which he sensed would be revealed to him at the proper time, and which he would not resist.

seven

Seven hours later, at the darkest hour of night, Mondschein knew that the time had come.

He woke, sweat-soaked, and slipped into his robe. The dormitory was silent. He left his room, glided quietly down the hall, entered the dropshaft. Moments later he emerged in the plaza fronting the dormitory buildings.

The night was cold. Here on the plateau the day's warmth fled swiftly once darkness descended. Shivering a little, Mondschein made his way through the streets of the center. No guards were on duty; there was no one to fear in this carefully selected, rigorously scanned colony of the faithful. Somewhere a watchful esper might be awake, seeking to detect hostile thoughts, but Mondschein was emanating nothing that might seem hostile. He did not know where he was going, nor what he was about to do. The forces that drove him welled from deep within his brain, beyond the fumbling reach of any esper. They guided his motor responses, not his cerebral centers.

He came to one of the information-retrieval centers, a stubby brick building with a blank windowless facade. Pressing his hand against the doorscanner, Mondschein waited to be identified; in a moment his pattern was checked against the master list of personnel, and he was admitted.

There flowered in his brain the knowledge of what he had come to find: a holographic camera.

They kept such equipment on the second level. Mondschein went to the storeroom, opened a cabinet, removed a compact object six inches square. Unhurriedly, he left the building, sliding the camera into his sleeve.

Crossing another plaza, Mondschein approached Lab XXIa, the longevity building. He had been there during the day, to give a biopsy. Now he moved briskly through the irising doorway, down a level into the basement, entered the small room just to his left. A rack of photomicrographs lay on a workbench along the rear wall. Mondschein touched a knuckle to the scanner-activator, and a conveyor belt dumped the photomicrographs into the hopper of a projector. They began to appear in the objective of the viewer.

Mondschein aimed his camera and made a hologram of each photomicrograph as it appeared. It was quick work. The camera's laser beam flicked out, bouncing off the subjects, rebounding and intersecting a second beam at 45 degrees. The holograms would be unrecognizable without the proper equipment for viewing; only a second laser beam, set at the same angle as the one with which the holograms had been taken, could transform the unrecognizable patterns of intersecting circles on the plates into images. Those images, Mondschein knew, would be three-dimensional and of extraordinarily fine resolution. But he did not stop to ponder on the use to which they might be put.

He moved through the laboratory, photographing everything that might be of some value. The camera could take hundreds of shots without recharging. Mondschein thumbed it again and again. Within two hours he had made a three-dimensional record of virtually the entire laboratory.

Shivering a little, he stepped out into the morning chill. Dawn was breaking. Mondschein put the camera back where he had found it, after removing the capsule of holographic plates. They were tiny; the whole capsule was not much bigger than a thumbnail. He slid it into his breast pocket and returned to the dormitory.

The moment his head touched the pillow, he forgot that he had left his room at all that night.

In the morning Mondschein said to Capodimonte, "Let's go to Frijoles today."

"You're really getting the bug, aren't you?" Capodimonte said, grinning.

Mondschein shrugged. "It's just a passing mood. I want to look at ruins, that's all."

"We could go to Puye, then. You haven't been there. It's pretty impressive, and quite different from—"

"No. Frijoles," Mondschein said. "All right?"

They got a permit to leave the center—it wasn't too difficult for lower-grade technicians to go out—and in the early part of the afternoon they headed westward toward the Indian ruins. The teardrop hummed along the road to Los Alamos, a secret scientific city of an earlier era, but they turned left into Bandelier National Monument before they reached Los Alamos, and bumped down an old asphalt road for a dozen miles until they came to the main center of the park.

It was never very crowded here, but now, with summer over, the place was all but deserted. The two acolytes strolled down the main path, past the circular canyon-bottom pueblo ruin known as Tyuonyi, carved from blocks of volcanic tuff, and up the winding little road that took them to the cave dwellings. When they reached the kiva, the hollowed-out chamber that once had been a ceremonial room for prehistoric Indians, Mondschein said, "Wait a minute. I want to have a look."

He scrambled up the wooden ladder and pulled himself into the kiva. Its walls were blackened by the smoke of ancient fires. Niches lined the wall where once had been stored objects of the highest ritual importance. Calmly and without really understanding what he was doing, Mondschein drew the tiny capsule of holograms from his pocket and placed it in an inconspicuous corner of the farthest left-hand niche. He spent another moment looking around the kiva, and emerged.

Capodimonte was sitting on the soft white rock at the base of the cliff, looking up at the high reddish wall on the far side of the canyon. Mondschein said, "Feel like taking a real hike today?"

"Where to? Frijolito Ruin?"

"No," Mondschein said. He pointed to the top of the canyon wall. "Out toward Yapashi. Or to the Stone Lions."

"That's a dozen miles," Capodimonte said. "And we hiked there in the middle of July. I'm not up to it again, Chris."

"Let's go back, then."

"You don't need to get angry," Capodimonte said. "Look, we can go to Ceremonial Cave instead. That's only a short hike. Enough's enough, Chris."

"All right," Mondschein said. "Ceremonial Cave it is."

He set the pace for the hike, and it was a brisk one. They had not gone a quarter of a mile before the pudgy Capodimonte was out of breath. Grimly, Mondschein forged on, Capodimonte straggling after him. They reached the ruin, viewed it briefly, and turned back. When they came to park headquarters, Capodimonte said that he wanted to rest awhile, to have a snack before returning to the research center.

"Go ahead," Mondschein said. "I'll browse in the curio shop."

He waited until Capodimonte was out of sight. Then, entering the curio shop, Mondschein went to the communibooth. A number popped into his brain, planted there hypnotically months before as he lay slumbering in the Nothing Chamber. He put money in the slot and punched out the number.

"Eternal Harmony," a voice answered.

"This is Mondschein. Let me talk to anybody in Section Thirteen."

"One moment, please."

Mondschein waited. His mind felt blank. He was a sleepwalker now.

A purring, breathy voice said, "Go ahead, Mondschein. Give us the details."

With great economy of words Mondschein told where he had hidden the capsule of holograms. The purring voice thanked him. Mondschein broke the contact and stepped from the booth. A few moments later Capodimonte entered the curio shop, looking fed and rested.

"See anything you want to buy?" he asked.

"No," Mondschein said. "Let's go."

Capodimonte drove. Mondschein eyed the scenery as it whizzed past, and drifted into deep contemplation. *Why did I come here today?* he wondered. He had no idea. He did not remember a thing—not a single detail of his espionage. The erasure had been complete.

eight

━━━━━━━━━━━━━━━━━

They came for him a week later, at midnight. A ponderous robot rumbled into his room without warning and took up a station beside his bed, the huge grips ready to seize him if he bolted. Accompanying the robot was a hatchet-faced little man named Magnus, one of the supervising Brothers of the center.

"What's happening?" Mondschein asked.

"Get dressed, spy. Come for interrogation."

"I'm no spy. There's a mistake, Brother Magnus."

"Save the arguments, Mondschein. Up. Get up. Don't attempt any violence."

Mondschein was mystified. But he knew better than to debate the matter with Magnus, especially with eight hundred pounds of lightning-fast metallic intelligence in the room. Puzzled, the acolyte quit his bed and slipped on a robe. He followed Magnus out. In the hallway others appeared and stared at him. There were guarded whispers.

Ten minutes later Mondschein found himself in a circular room on the fifth floor of the research center's main administration building, surrounded by more Brotherhood brass than he had ever expected to see in one room. There were eight of them, all high in councils. A knot of tension coiled in Mondschein's belly. Light glared into his eyes.

"The esper's here," someone muttered.

They had sent a girl, no more than sixteen, pasty-faced and plain. Her skin was flecked with small red blotches. Her eyes were alert, unpleasantly gleaming, never still.

Mondschein despised her on sight, and he tried desperately to keep the emotion under rein, knowing that she could seal his fate with a word. It was no use: she detected his contempt for her the moment she came into the room, and the fleshy lips moved in a quick twitching smile. She drew her dumpy body erect.

Supervisor Magnus said, "This is the man. What do you read in him?"

"Fear. Hatred. Defiance."

"How about disloyalty?"

"His highest loyalty is to himself," the esper said, clasping her hands complacently over her belly.

"Has he betrayed us?" Magnus demanded.

"No. I don't see anything that says he has."

Mondschein said, "If I could ask the meaning of—"

"Quiet," Magnus said witheringly.

Another of the Supervisors said, "The evidence is incontrovertible. Perhaps the girl's making a mistake."

"Scan him more closely," Magnus directed. "Go back, day by day, through his memory. Don't miss a thing. You know what you're looking for."

Baffled, Mondschein looked in appeal at the steely faces about him. The girl seemed to be gloating. *Stinking voyeur,* he thought. *Have a good scan!*

The girl said thinly, "He thinks I'm going to enjoy this. He ought to try swimming through a cesspool sometime, if he wants to know what it's like."

"Scan him," Magnus said. "It's late and we have many questions to answer."

She nodded. Mondschein waited for some sensation telling him that his memories were being probed, some feeling as of invisible fingers going through his brain. There was no such awareness. Long moments passed in silence, and then the girl looked up in triumph.

"The night of March thirteenth's been erased."

"Can you get beneath the erasure?" Magnus asked.

"Impossible. It's an expert job. They've cut the whole night right out of him. And they've loaded him with countermnemonics all the way down the track. He doesn't know a thing about what he's been up to," the girl said.

The Supervisors exchanged glances. Mondschein felt perspiration soaking through his robe. The smell of it stung his nostrils. A muscle throbbed in his cheek, and his forehead itched murderously, but he did not move.

"She can go," Magnus said.

With the esper out of the room, the atmosphere grew a little less tense, but Mondschein did not relax. In a bleak, hopeless way, he felt that he had been tried and condemned in advance for a crime whose nature he did not even know. He thought of some of the perhaps apocryphal stories of Brotherhood vindictiveness: the man with the pain centers removed, the esper staked out to endure an overload, the lobotomized biologist, the renegade Supervisor who was left in a Nothing Chamber for ninety-six consecutive hours. He realized that he might find out very shortly just how apocryphal those stories were.

Magnus said, "For your information, Mondschein, someone broke into the longevity lab and shot the whole place up with a holograph. It was a very neat job, except that we've got an alarm system in there, and you happened to trip it."

"Sir, I swear, I never set foot inside—"

"Save it, Mondschein. The morning after, we ran a neutron activation analysis in there, just as a matter of routine. We turned up traces of tungsten and molybdenum that brushed off you while you were taking those holograms. They match your skin pattern. It took us awhile to track them to you. There's no doubt—same neutron pattern on the camera, on the lab equipment, and on your hand. You were sent in here as a spy, whether you know it or not."

Another Supervisor said, "Kirby's here."

"I'd like to know what he's got to say about this," Magnus muttered darkly.

Mondschein saw the lean, long-limbed figure of Reynolds Kirby enter the room. His thin lips were clamped tightly together. He seemed to have aged at least ten years since Mondschein had seen him in Langholt's office.

Magnus whirled and said with open irritation, "Here's your man, Kirby. What do you think of him now?"

"He's not my man," said Kirby.

"You approved his transfer here," Magnus snapped. "Maybe we ought to run a scan on you, eh? Somebody worked a loaded bomb into this place, and the bomb's gone off. He handed a whole laboratory away."

"Maybe not," Kirby said. "Maybe he's still got the data on him somewhere."

"He was out of the center the day after the laboratory was entered. He and another acolyte went to visit some ancient Indian ruins. It's a safe bet that he disposed of the holograms while he was out there."

"Have you tracked the courier?" Kirby asked.

"We're getting away from the point," said Magnus. "The point is that this man came to the center on your recommendation. You picked him out of nowhere and put him here. What we'd all like to know is where you found him and why you sent him here. Eh?"

Kirby's fleshless face worked wordlessly for a moment. He glowered at Mondschein, then stared in even greater hostility at Magnus. At length he said, "I can't take responsibility for shipping this man here. It happens that he wrote to me in February, asking to be transferred out of normal chapel duties and sent here. He was going over the heads of his local administrators, so I sent the letter back suggesting that he be disciplined a little. A few weeks later I received instructions that he be transferred out here. I was startled, to say the least, but I approved them. That's all I know about Christopher Mondschein."

Magnus extended a forefinger and tapped the air. "Wait one moment, Kirby. You're a Supervisor. Who gives you instructions, anyway? How can you be pressured into making a transfer when you're in high authority?"

"The instructions came from higher authority."

"I find that hard to believe," Magnus said.

Mondschein sat stock-still, enthralled despite his own predicament by this battle between Supervisors. He had never understood how he had managed to get that transfer, and now it began to seem as though no one else understood it, either.

Kirby said, "The instructions came from a source I'm reluctant to name."

"Covering up for yourself, Kirby?"

"You're taking liberties with my patience, Supervisor Magnus," said Kirby tightly.

"I want to know who put this spy among us."

Kirby took a deep breath. "All right," he said. "I'll tell you. All of you be my witness to this. The order came from Vorst. Noel Vorst called me and said he wanted this man sent here. Vorst sent him. *Vorst!* What do you make of that?"

nine

They were not finished interrogating Mondschein. Waves of espers worked him over, trying to get beneath the erasure, without success. Organic methods were employed, too: Mondschein was shot full of truth serums old and new, everything from sodium pentothal on up, and batteries of hard-faced Brothers questioned him rigorously. Mondschein let them strip his soul bare, so that every bit of nastiness, every self-seeking moment, everything that made him a human being stood out in bold relief. They found nothing useful. Nor did a four-hour immersion in a Nothing Chamber yield results; Mondschein was too wobbly-brained to be able to answer questions for three days afterward, that was all.

He was as puzzled as they were. He would gladly have confessed the most heinous of sins; in fact, several times during the long interrogation he *did* confess, simply to have it over with, but the espers read his motives plainly and laughed his confessions to scorn. Somehow, he knew, he had fallen into the hands of the enemies of the Brotherhood and had concluded a pact with them, a pact which he had fulfilled. But he had no inner knowledge of any of that. Whole segments of his memory were gone, and that was terrifying to him.

Mondschein knew that he was finished. They would not let him remain at Santa Fe, naturally. His dream of being on hand when immortality was achieved now was ended. They would cast him out with flaming swords, and he would wither and grow old, cursing his lost opportunity. That is, if they did not kill him outright or work some subtle form of slow destruction on him.

A light December snow was falling on the day that Supervisor Kirby came to tell him his fate.

"You can go, Mondschein," the tall man said somberly.

"Go? Where?"

"Wherever you like. Your case has been decided. You're guilty, but there's reasonable doubt of your volition. You're being expelled from the Brotherhood, but otherwise no action will be taken against you."

"Does that mean I'm expelled from the church as a communicant, too?"

"Not necessarily. That's up to you. If you want to come to worship, we won't deny our comfort to you," Kirby said. "But there's no possibility of your holding a position within the church. You've been tampered with, and we can't take further chances with you. I'm sorry, Mondschein."

Mondschein was sorry, too, but relieved, as well. They would not take revenge on him. He would lose nothing but his chance at life everlasting—and perhaps he would even retain that, just as any other common worshiper did.

He had forfeited, of course, his chance to rise in the Vorster hierarchy. But there was another hierarchy, too, Mondschein thought, where a man might move more swiftly.

The Brotherhood took him to the city of Santa Fe proper, gave him some money, and turned him loose. Mondschein headed immediately for the nearest chapel of the Transcendent Harmony, which turned out to be in Albuquerque, twenty minutes away.

"We've been expecting you," a Harmonist in flowing green robes told him. "I've got instructions to contact my superiors the moment you show up."

Mondschein was not surprised at that. Nor was he greatly astonished to be told, a short while later, that he was to leave by quickboat for Rome right away. The Harmonists would pay his expenses, he was informed.

A slim woman with surgically-altered eyelids met him at the station in Rome. She did not look familiar to him, but she smiled at him as though they were old friends. She conveyed him to a house on the Via Flaminia, a few dozen miles north of Rome, where a squat, sallow-faced Harmonist Brother with a bulbous nose awaited him.

"Welcome," the Harmonist said. "Do you remember me?"

"No, I—yes. *Yes!*"

Recollection flooded back, dizzying him, staggering him. There had been three heretics in the room that other time, not just one, and they had given him wine and promised him a place in the Harmonist hierarchy, and he had agreed to let himself be smuggled into Santa Fe, a soldier in the great crusade, a warrior of light, a Harmonist spy.

"You did very well, Mondschein," the heretic said unctuously. "We didn't think you'd be caught so fast, but we weren't sure of all their detection methods. We could only guard against the espers, and we did a fair enough job of that. At any rate, the information you provided was extremely useful."

"And you'll keep your end of the bargain? I'm to get a tenth-level job?"

"Of course. You didn't think we'd cheat you, did you? You'll have a three-month indoctrination course so you can attain insight into our movement. Then you'll assume your new duties in our organization. Which would you prefer, Mondschein—Mars or Venus?"

"Mars or Venus? I don't follow you."

"We're going to attach you to our missionary division. You'll be leaving Earth by next summer, to carry on our work in one of the colonies. You're free to choose the one you prefer."

Mondschein was aghast. He had never bargained for this. Selling out to these heretics, only to get shipped off to an alien world and likely martyrdom—no, he had never expected anything like that.

Faust didn't expect his troubles, either, Mondschein thought coldly.

He said, "What kind of trick is this? You've got no right to ask me to become a missionary!"

"We offered you a tenth-level job," the Harmonist said quietly. "The option of choosing the division it would be remained with us."

Mondschein was silent. There was a fierce throbbing in his skull. The face of the Harmonist seemed to blur and waver. He was free to leave—to step out the door and merge into the multitudes. To become nothing. Or he could submit and be—what? Anything. Anything.

Dead in six weeks, as likely as not.

"I'll take it," he said. "Venus. I'll go to Venus." His words sounded like a cage clanging shut.

The Harmonist nodded. "I thought you would," he said. He turned to leave, then paused and stared curiously at Mondschein. "Did you really think you could name your own position—*spy*?"

THREE
Where the Changed Ones Go
2135

one

The Venusian boy danced nimbly around the patch of Trouble Fungus behind the chapel, avoiding the gray-green killer with practiced ease. He hop-skipped past the rubbery bole of the Limblime Tree and approached the serried row of jagged nameless stalks that lined the back garden. The boy grinned at them, and they parted for him as obligingly as the Red Sea had yielded to Moses some time earlier.

"Here I am," he said to Nicholas Martell.

"I didn't think you'd be back," the Vorster missionary said.

The boy—Elwhit—looked mischievous. "Brother Christopher said I couldn't come back. That's why I'm here. Tell me about the Blue Fire. Can you really make atoms give light?"

"Come inside," Martell said.

The boy represented his first triumph since coming to Venus, and a small triumph it was, so far. But Martell did not object to that. A step was a step. There was a planet to win here. A universe to win, perhaps.

Inside the chapel the boy hung back, suddenly shy. He was no more than ten, Martell guessed. Was it just wickedness that had made him come here? Or was he a spy from the chapel of heretics down the road? No matter. Martell would treat him as a potential convert. He activated the altar, and the Blue Fire welled into the small room, colors dancing against the boards of the groined wooden ceiling. Power surged from the cobalt cube, and the harmless, dramatic radiations wrung a gasp of awe from Elwhit.

"The fire is symbolic," Martell murmured. "There's an underlying oneness in the universe—the common building blocks, do you see? Do you know what atomic particles are? Protons, electrons, neutrons? The things everything's made up of?"

"I can touch them," Elwhit said. "I can push them around."

"Will you show me how?" Martell was remembering the way the boy had parted those knifeblade-sharp plants in back. A glance, a mental shove, and they had yielded. These Venusians could teleport—he was sure of it. "How do you push things?" Martell asked.

But the boy shrugged the question aside. "Tell me more about the Blue Fire," he said.

"Have you read the book I gave you? The one by Vorst? That tells you all you need to know."

"Brother Christopher took it away from me."

"You showed it to him?" Martell said, startled.

"He wanted to know why I came to you. I said you talked to me and gave me a book. He took the book. I came back. Tell me why you're here. Tell me what you teach."

Martell hadn't imagined that his first convert would be a child. He said carefully, "The religion we have here is very much like the one that Brother Christopher teaches. But there are some differences. His people make up a lot of stories. They're good stories, but they're only stories."

"About Lazarus, you mean?"

"That's right. Myths, nothing more. We try not to need such things. We're trying to get right in touch with the basics of the universe. We—"

The boy lost interest. He tugged at his tunic and nudged at a chair. The altar was what fascinated him, nothing else. The glistening eyes roved toward it.

Martell said, "The cobalt is radioactive. It's a source of betas—electrons. They're going through the tank and knocking photons loose. That's where the light comes from."

"I can stop the light," the boy said. "Will you be angry if I stop it?"

It was a kind of sacrilege, Martell knew. But he suspected that he would be forgiven. Any evidence of teleporting activity that he could gather was useful.

"Go ahead," he said.

The boy remained motionless. But the radiance dimmed. It was as if an invisible hand reached into the reactor, intercepting the darting particles. Telekinesis on the subatomic level! Martell was elated and chilled all at once, watching the light fade. Suddenly it flared more brightly again. Beads of sweat glistened on the boy's bluish-purple forehead.

"That is all," Elwhit announced.

"How do you do it?"

"I reach." He laughed. "You can't?"

"Afraid not," Martell said. "Listen, if I give you another book to read, will you promise not to show it to Brother Christopher? I don't have many. I can't afford to have the Harmonists confiscate them all."

"Next time," the boy said. "I don't feel like reading things now. I'll come again. You tell me all about it some other time."

He danced away, out of the chapel, and went skipping through the underbrush, heedless of the perils that lurked in the deep-shadowed forest beyond. Martell watched him go, not knowing whether he was actually making his first convert or whether he was being mocked.

Perhaps both, the missionary thought.

Nicholas Martell had come to Venus ten days before, aboard a passenger ship from Mars. He had been one of thirty passengers aboard the ship, but none of the others had cared for Nicholas Martell's company. Ten of them were Martians, who did not care to share the atmosphere Martell breathed. Martians, now that their planet had been cozily Terraformed, preferred to fill their lungs with an Earthside mix of gases. So had Martell, once, for he was a native Earthman himself. But now he was one of the changed ones, equipped with gills in good Venusian fashion.

Not gills, truly: they would serve no function under water. They were high-density filters, to strain the molecules of decent oxygen from the Venusian air. Martell was well adapted. His metabolism had no use for helium or the other inerts, but it could draw sustenance from nitrogen and had no real objections to fueling on CO_2 for short spells. The surgeons at Santa Fe had worked on him for six months. It was forty years too late to make adjustments on Martell-ovum or Martell-fetus, as was the normal practice in fitting a man for life on Venus, so they had done their work on Martell the man. The blood that flowed in his veins was no longer red. His skin had a fine cyanotic flush. He was as a Venusian born.

There had been nineteen Venusians of the true blood aboard the ship, too. But they felt no kinship for Martell and had forced him to withdraw from their presence. The crewmen had set up Martell's cradle in a storage chamber, with gentle apologies: "You know those arrogant Venusians, Brother. Give them the wrong kind of look and they're at you with their daggers. You'll stay here. You'll be safer here." A thin laugh. "You'll be even safer, Brother, if you head for home without ever setting foot on Venus."

Martell had smiled. He was prepared to let Venus do its worst.

Venus had martyred several dozen members of Martell's religious order in the past forty years. He was a Vorster, or, more formally, a member of the Brotherhood of the Immanent Radiance, and he had attached himself to the missionary wing. Unlike his martyred predecessors, Martell was surgically adapted to live on Venus. The others had had to muffle themselves in breathing-suits, and perhaps that had limited their effectiveness. The Vorsters had made no headway on Venus at all, though they were the dominant religious group on Earth, and had been for more than a generation. Martell, alone and adapted, had taken upon himself the long-delayed task of founding a Venusian order of the Brotherhood.

Martell had had a chilly welcome from Venus. He had blanked out in the turbulence of the landing as the ship plunged through the cloud layer. Then he had recovered. He sat patiently, a thin man with a wedge-shaped face and pale, hooded eyes. Through the port he had his first glimpse of Venus: a flat, muddy-looking field, stretching perhaps half a mile, with a bordering fringe of thick-trunked, ugly trees whose massed bluish leaves had a sinister glint. The sky was gray, and swirling clumps of low-lying clouds formed whorling patterns against the deeper background. Robot technicians were bustling from a squat, alien-looking building to service the ship's needs. The passengers were coming forth.

In the landing station a low-caste Venusian stared at the Vorster with blank indifference, taking his passport and saying coolly, "Religious?"

"That's right."

"How'd you get in?"

"Treaty of 2128," Martell said. "A limited quota of Earthside observers for scientific, ethical, or—"

"Spare me." The Venusian pressed his fingertip to a page of the passport and a visa stamp appeared, glowing brilliantly. "Nicholas Martell. You'll die here, Martell. Why don't you go back where you came from? Men live forever there, don't they?"

"They live a long time. But I have work here."

"Fool!"

"Perhaps," Martell agreed calmly. "May I go?"

"Where are you staying? We have no hotels here."

"The Martian Embassy will look after me until I'm established."

"You'll never be established," the Venusian said.

Martell did not contradict him. He knew that even a low-caste Venusian regarded himself as superior to an Earthman, and that a contradiction might seem a mortal insult. Martell was not equipped for dagger-dueling. And, since he was not a proud man by nature, he was willing to swallow any manner of abuse for the sake of his mission.

The passport man waved him on. Martell gathered up his single suitcase and passed out of the building. *A taxi now,* he thought. It was many miles to town. He needed to rest and to confer with the Martian Ambassador, Weiner. The Martians were not particularly sympathetic to his aims, but at least they were willing to countenance Martell's presence here. There was no Earth Embassy, not even a consulate. The links between the mother planet and her proud colony had been broken long ago.

Taxis waited at the far side of the field. Martell began to cross to them. The ground crunched beneath his feet, as though it were only a brittle crust. The planet looked gloomy. Not a hint of sun came through those clouds. His adapted body was functioning well, though.

The spaceport, Martell thought, had a forlorn look. Hardly anyone but robots seemed to be about. A staff of four Venusians ran the place, and there were the nineteen from his ship, and the ten Martians, but no one else. Venus was a sparsely populated planet, with hardly more than three million people in its seven widely spaced towns. The Venusians were frontiersmen, legendary for their haughtiness. They had room to be haughty, Martell thought. Let them spend a week on teeming Earth and they might change their ways.

"Taxi!" Martell called.

None of the robocars budged from their line. Were even the robots haughty here, he wondered? Or was there something wrong with his accent? He called again, getting no response.

Then he understood. The Venusian passengers were emerging and crossing to the taxi zone. And, naturally, they had precedence. Martell watched them. They were high-caste men, unlike the passport man. They walked with an arrogant, swaggering gait, and Martell knew they would slash him to his knees if he crossed their path.

He felt a bit of contempt for them. What were they, anyway, but blue-skinned samurai, border lairds after their proper time, childish, self-appointed princelings living a medieval fantasy? Men who were sure of themselves did not need to swagger, nor to surround themselves with elaborate codes of chivalry. If one looked upon them as uneasy, inwardly uncertain hotheads, rather than as innately superior noblemen, one could surmount the feeling of awe that a procession of them provoked.

And yet one could not entirely suppress that awe.

For they *were* impressive as they paraded across the field. More than custom separated the high-caste and the low-caste Venusians. They were biologically different. The high-caste ones were the first comers, the founding families of the Venus colony, and they were far more alien in body and mind than Venusians of more recent vintage. The early genetic processes had been unsubtle, and the first colonists had been transformed virtually into monsters. Close to eight feet tall, with dark blue skins pocked with giant pores, and pendulous red gill-bunches at their throats, they were alien beings who gave little sign that they were the great-great-grandchildren of Earthmen. Later in the process of colonizing Venus, it had become possible to adapt men for the second planet without varying nearly so much from the basic human model. Both strains of Venusians, since they arose from manipulation of the germ plasm, bred true; both shared the same exaggerated sense of honor and the same disdain for Earth; both were now alien strains, inwardly and outwardly, in mind and in body. But those whose ancestry went back to the most changed of the changed ones were in charge, making a virtue of their strangeness, and the planet was their playground.

Martell watched as the high-caste ones solemnly entered the waiting vehicles and drove off. No taxis remained. The ten Martian passengers of the ship could be seen getting into a cab on the other side of the depot. Martell returned to the building. The low-caste Venusian glowered at him.

Martell said, "When will I be able to get a taxi to town?"

"You won't. They aren't coming back today."

"I want to call the Martian Embassy, then. They'll send a car for me."

"Are you sure they will? Why should they bother?"

"Perhaps so," Martell said evenly. "I'd better walk."

The look he got from the Venusian was worth the gesture. The man stared in surprise and shock. And, possibly, admiration, mingled somewhat with patronizing confidence that Martell must be a madman. Martell left the station. He began to walk, following the narrow ribbon of a road, letting the unearthly atmosphere soak deep into his altered body.

two

It was a lonely walk. Not a sign of habitation broke the belt of vegetation on either side of the highway, nor did any vehicles pass him. The trees, somber and eerie with their bluish cast, towered over the road. Their knifeblade-like leaves glimmered in the faint, diffused light. There was an occasional rustling sound in the woods, as of beasts crashing through the thickets. Martell saw nothing there, though. He walked on. How many miles? Eight, a dozen? He was prepared to walk forever, if necessary. He had the strength.

His mind hummed with plans. He would establish a small chapel and let it be known what the Brotherhood had to offer: life eternal and the key to the stars. The Venusians might threaten to kill him, as they had killed previous missionaries of the Brotherhood, but Martell was prepared to die, if necessary, that others might have the stars. His faith was strong. Before his departure the high ones of the Brotherhood had personally wished him well: grizzled Reynolds Kirby, the Hemispheric Coordinator, had grasped his hand, and then had come an even greater surprise as Noel Vorst himself, the Founder, a legendary figure more than a century old, had come forth to tell him in a soft, feathery voice, "I know that your mission will bear fruit, Brother Martell."

Martell still tingled with the memory of that glorious moment.

Now he strode forward, buoyed by the sight of a few habitations set back from the road. He was at the outskirts, then. On this pioneer world, pioneer habits held true, and the colonists did not build their homes close together. They spread sparsely over a radiating area surrounding the main administrative centers. The man-high walls enclosing the first houses he saw did not surprise him; these Venusians were a surly lot who would build a wall around their entire planet if they could. But soon he would be in town, and then—

Martell came to a halt as he saw the Wheel hurtling toward him.

His first thought was that it had broken free from some vehicle. Then he realized what it was: no fragment of machinery, but Venusian wildlife. It surged over a crest in the road, a hundred yards in front of him, and came plunging wildly toward him at what must have been a speed of ninety miles an hour. Martell had a clear though momentary glimpse: two wheels of some horny substance, mottled orange and yellow, linked by a box-like inner structure. The wheels were nine feet across, at least; the connecting structure was smaller, so that wheel-rims projected around it. Those rims were razor-sharp. The creature moved by ceaselessly transferring its weight within that central housing, and it developed terrific momentum as it barreled toward the missionary.

Martell leaped back. The Wheel hurtled past him, missing his toes by inches. Martell saw the sharpness of the rim and felt an acrid odor sting his nostrils. If he had been a bit slower, the Wheel would have sliced him in two.

It traveled a hundred yards beyond him. Then, like a gyroscope running amok, it executed a turn in an astonishingly narrow radius and came shooting back toward Martell.

The thing's hunting me, he thought.

He knew many Vorster combat techniques, but none of them were designed to cope with a beast like this. All he could do was keep sidestepping and hope that the Wheel could not make sudden compensations in its course. It drew near; Martell sucked in his breath and leaped back once again. This time the Wheel swerved ever so slightly.

Its leading left-hand edge sliced through the trailing end of Martell's blue cloak, and a ribbon of cloth fluttered to the pavement. Panting, Martell watched the thing swing around for another try, and knew that it could indeed correct its course. A few more passes and it would split him.

The Wheel came a third time.

Martell waited as long as he dared. With the outer blades only a few feet away, he broad-jumped—into the path of the creature. Earthborn muscles carried him twenty feet in the light gravity. He more than half expected to be bisected in mid-jump, but when his feet touched ground he was still in one piece. Whirling, Martell saw that he had indeed surprised the beast; it had turned inward, toward the place where it had expected him to be, and had passed through his suitcase. The suitcase had been sliced as though by a laser beam. His belongings were scattered on the road. The Wheel, halting once more, was coming back for another try.

What now? Climb a tree? The nearest one was void of limbs for the first twenty feet. Martell could not shinny to safety in time. All he could do was keep hopping from side to side in the road, trying to outguess the creature. He knew that he could not keep that up much longer. He would tire, and the Wheel would not, and the slashing rims would pass through him and spill his altered guts on the pavement. It did not seem right, Martell thought, to die purposelessly in this way before he had even begun his work here.

The Wheel came. Martell sidestepped it again and heard it whistle past. Was it getting angry? No, it was just an insensate brute looking for a meal, hunting in the manner some perverse nature had designed for it. Martell gasped for breath. On the next pass—

Suddenly he was not alone. A boy appeared, running out from one of the stockaded buildings at the crest of the hill, and trotted alongside the Wheel for a few paces. Then—Martell did not see how it was done—the Wheel went awry and toppled, landing on one disk with the other in the air. It lay there like a huge cheese blocking the road. The boy, who could not have been much more than ten, stood by it, looking pleased with himself. He was low-caste, of course. A high-caste one would not have bothered to save him. Martell realized that probably the low-caste boy had had no interest in saving him, either, but simply had knocked the Wheel over for the sport of it.

Martell said, "I offer thanks, friend. Another moment and I'd have been cut to ribbons."

The boy made no reply. Martell came closer to inspect the fallen Wheel. Its upper rim was rippling in frustration as it strained to right itself—clearly an impossible task. Martell looked down, saw a dark violet cyst near the center of one wheel writhe and open.

"Look out!" the boy cried, but it was much too late.

Two whip-like threads burst from the cyst. One wrapped itself around Martell's left thigh, the other around the boy's waist. Martell felt a blaze of pain, as though the threads were lined with acid-edged suckers. A mouth opened on the inner structure of the Wheel. Martell saw milling, grinding tooth-like projections beginning to churn in anticipation.

But this was a situation he could handle. He had no way of stopping the headlong plunge of the Wheel, for that was mere mechanical energy at work, but presumably the creature's brain carried an electrical charge, and the Vorsters had ways of altering current flows in the brain. It was a mild form of esping, within the threshold of nearly anyone who cared to master the disciplines involved. Ignoring the pain, Martell seized the tightening thread with his right hand and performed the act of neutralization. A moment later the thread went slack and Martell was free. So was the boy. The threads did not return to the cyst, but remained lying limp in the roadway. The milling teeth became still; the rippling horny plate of the upper wheel subsided. The thing was dead.

Martell glanced at the boy.

"Fair enough," he said. "I've saved you and you've saved me. So now we're even."

"The debit is still yours," replied the boy with strange solemnity. "If I had not rescued you first, you never would have lived to rescue me. And it would not have been necessary to rescue me, anyway, since I would not have come out onto the road, and therefore—"

Martell's eyes widened. "Who taught you to reason like that?" he asked in amusement. "You sound like a theology professor."

"I am Brother Christopher's pupil."

"And he is—"

"You'll find out. He wants to see you. He sent me out here to fetch you."

"And where will I find him?"

"Come with me."

Martell followed the boy toward one of the buildings. They left the dead Wheel in the road; Martell wondered what would happen if a carload of high-casters came along and had to shove the carcass out of the way with their own aristocratic hands.

Martell and the boy passed through a burnished coppery gate that slid open at the boy's approach. Martell found himself approaching a simple wooden A-frame building. When he saw the sign mounted above the door, he was so amazed that he released his grip on his sundered suitcase, and for the second time in ten minutes his belongings went spilling to the ground.

The sign said:

SHRINE OF THE TRANSCENDENT HARMONY
ALL ARE WELCOME

Martell's knees felt watery. Harmonists? *Here?*

The green-robed heretics, offshoots of the original Vorster movement, had made some progress on Earth for a while, and had even seemed to threaten the parent organization. But for more than twenty years now they had been nothing but an absurd little splinter group of no significance. It was inconceivable that these heretics, who had failed so utterly on Earth, could have established a church here on Venus—something that the Vorsters themselves had been unable to do. It was impossible. It was unthinkable.

A figure appeared in the doorway—a stocky man in early middle age, about sixty or so, his hair beginning to gray, his features thickening. Like Martell, he had been surgically adapted to Venusian conditions. He looked calm and self-assured. His hands rested lightly on a comfortable priestly paunch.

He said, "I'm Christopher Mondschein. I heard of your arrival, Brother Martell. Won't you come in?"

Martell hesitated.

Mondschein smiled. "Come, come, Brother. There's no peril in breaking bread with a Harmonist, is there? You'd be mincemeat now but for the lad's bravery, and I sent him to save you. You owe me the courtesy of a visit. Come in. Come in. I won't meddle with your soul, Brother. That's a promise."

three

The Harmonist place was unassuming but obviously permanent. There was a shrine, festooned with the statuettes and claptrap of the heresy, and a library, and dwelling quarters. Martell caught sight of several Venusian boys at work in the rear of the building, digging what might be the foundations of an extension. Martell followed the older man into the library. A familiar row of books caught his eye: the works of Noel Vorst, handsomely bound, the expensive Founder's Edition.

Mondschein said, "Are you surprised? Don't forget that we accept the supremacy of Vorst, too, even if he spurns us. Sit down. Wine? They make a fine dry white here."

"What are you doing here?" Martell asked.

"Me? That's a terribly long story, and not entirely creditable to me. The essence of it is that I was a young fool and let myself get maneuvered into being sent here. That was forty years ago, and I've stopped resenting what happened by now. It was the finest thing that could have happened to me in my life, I've come to realize, and I suppose it's a mark of maturity that I was able to see—"

Mondschein's garrulity irritated the precise-minded Martell. He cut in: "I don't want your personal history, Brother Mondschein. I meant, how long has your order been here?"

"Close to fifty years."

"Uninterruptedly?"

"Yes. We have eight shrines here and about four

thousand communicants, all of them low-caste. The high-casters don't deign to notice us."

"They don't deign to wipe you out, either," Martell observed.

"True," said Mondschein. "Perhaps we're beneath their contempt."

"But they've killed every Vorster missionary who's ever come here," Martell said. "Us they devour, you they tolerate. Why is that?"

"Perhaps they see a strength in us that they don't find in the parent organization," suggested the heretic. "They admire strength, of course. You must know that, or you'd never have tried to walk from the landing station. You were demonstrating your strength under stress. But of course it would rather have spoiled your demonstration if that Wheel had slashed you to death."

"As it very nearly did."

"As it certainly would have done," said Mondschein, "if I had not happened to notice your predicament. That would have terminated your mission here rather prematurely. Do you like the wine?"

Martell had barely tasted it. "It's not bad. Tell me, Mondschein, have they really let themselves be converted here?"

"A few. A few."

"Hard to believe. What do you people know that we don't?"

"It isn't what we know," Mondschein said. "It's what we have to offer. Come with me into the chapel."

"I'd rather not."

"Please. It won't give you a disease."

Reluctantly, Martell allowed himself to be led right into the sanctum sanctorum. He looked around with distaste at the ikons, the images, and all the rest of the Harmonist rubbish. At the altar, where a Vorster chapel would have had the tiny reactor emitting blue Cerenkov radiation, there was mounted a gleaming atom-symbol model along which electron-simulacra pulsed in blinding, ceaseless motion. Martell did not think of himself as a bigoted man, but he was loyal to his faith, and the sight of all this childish paraphernalia sickened him.

Mondschein said, "Noel Vorst's the most brilliant man of our times, and his accomplishments mustn't be underrated. He saw the culture of Earth fragmented and decadent, saw people everywhere escaping into drug addictions and Nothing Chambers and a hundred other deplorable things. And he saw that the old religions had lost their grip, that the time was ripe for an eclectic, synthetic new creed that dispensed with the mysticism of the former religions and replaced it with a new kind of mysticism, a scientific mysticism. That Blue Fire of his—a wonderful symbol, something to capture the imagination and dazzle the eye, as good as the Cross and the Crescent, even better, because it was modern, it was scientific, it could be comprehended even while it bewildered. Vorst had the insight to establish his cult and the administrative ability to put it across. But has thinking was incomplete."

"That's a lofty dismissal, isn't it? When you consider that we control Earth in a way that no single religious movement of the past has ever—"

Mondschein smiled. "The achievement on Earth is very imposing, I agree. Earth was ready for Vorst's doctrines. Why did he fail on the other planets, though? Because his thinking was too advanced. He didn't offer anything that colonists could surrender their hearts and souls to."

"He offers physical immortality in the present body," Martell said crisply. "Isn't that enough?"

"No. He doesn't offer a mythos. Just a cold quid-pro-quo, come to the chapel and pay your tithe and you can live forever, maybe. It's a secular religion, despite all the litanies and rituals that have been creeping in. It lacks poetry. There's no Christ-child in the manger, no Abraham sacrificing Isaac, no spark of humanity, no—"

"No simplistic fairy tales," said Martell in a brusque tone. "Agreed. That's the whole point of our teaching. We came into a world no longer capable of believing the old stories, and instead of spinning new ones we offered simplicity, strength, the power of scientific achievement—"

"And took political control of most of the planet, while

also establishing magnificent laboratories that carried on advanced research in longevity and esping. Fine. Fine. Admirable. But you failed here. We are succeeding. We have a story to tell, the story of Noel Vorst, the First Immortal, his redemption in the atomic fire, his awakening from sin. We offer our people a chance to be redeemed in Vorst and in the later prophet of Transcendent Harmony, David Lazarus. What we have is something that captures the fancy of the low-casters, and in another generation we'll have the high-casters, too. These are pioneers, Brother Martell. They've cut all ties with Earth, and they're starting over on their own, in a society just a few generations old. They need myths. They're shaping myths of their own here. Don't you think that in another century the first colonists of Venus will be regarded as supernatural beings, Martell? *Don't you think that they'll be Harmonist saints by then?"*

Martell was genuinely startled. "Is that your game?"

"Part of it."

"All you're doing is returning to fifth-century Christianity."

"Not exactly. We're continuing the scientific work, too."

"And you believe your own teachings?" Martell asked.

Mondschein smiled strangely. "When I was young," he said, "I was a Vorster acolyte, at the Nyack chapel. I went into the Brotherhood because it was a job. I needed a structure for my life, and I had a wild hope of being sent out to Santa Fe to become a subject in the immortality experiments, and so I enrolled. For the most unworthy of motives. Do you know, Martell, that I didn't feel a shred of a religious calling? Not even the Vorster stuff—stripped down, secular—could get to me. Through a series of confusions that I still don't fully understand and that I won't even begin to explain to you, I left the Brotherhood and joined the Harmonist movement and came here as a missionary. The most successful missionary ever sent to Venus, as it happens. Do you think the Harmonist mythologies can move me if I was too rational to accept Vorster thinking?"

"So you're completely cynical in handing out this nonsense about saints and images. You do it for the sake of preserving your power. A peddler of nostrums, a quack preacher in the backwoods of Venus—"

"Easy," Mondschein warned. "I'm getting results. And, as I think Noel Vorst himself might tell you, we deal in ends, not in means. Would you like to kneel here and pray awhile?"

"Of course not."

"May I pray for you, then?"

"You just told me you don't believe your own creed."

Smiling, Mondschein said, "Even the prayers of an unbeliever may be heard. Who knows? Only one thing is certain: you'll die here, Martell. So I'll pray for you, that you may pass through the purifying flame of the higher frequencies."

"Spare me. Why are you so sure I'll die here? It's a fallacy to assume that, simply because all previous Vorster missionaries have been martyred here, I'll be martyred, too."

"Our own position is uneasy enough on Venus. Yours will be impossible. Venus doesn't want you. Shall I tell you the only way you'll possibly live more than a month here?"

"Do."

"Join us. Trade in that blue tunic for a green one. We have need for all the capable men we can get."

"Don't be absurd. Do you really think I'd do any such thing?"

"It isn't beyond possibility. Many men have left your order for mine—myself included."

"I prefer martyrdom," Martell said.

"In what way will that benefit anybody? Be reasonable, Brother. Venus is a fascinating place. Wouldn't you like to live to see a little of it? Join us. You'll learn the rituals soon enough. You'll see that we aren't such ogres. And—"

"Thank you," said Martell. "Will you excuse me now?"

"I had hoped you would be our guest for dinner."

"That won't be possible. I'm expected at the Martian

Embassy, if I don't meet any more local beasts in the road."

Mondschein looked unruffled by Martell's rejection of his offer—an offer that could not have been made, Martell thought, in any great degree of seriousness. The older man said gravely, "Allow me, at least, to offer you transportation to town. Surely your pride in your own sanctity will permit you to accept that."

Martell smiled. "Gladly. It'll make a good story to tell Coordinator Kirby—how the heretics saved my life and gave me a ride into town."

"After making an attempt to seduce you from your faith."

"Naturally. May I leave now?"

"It'll be a few moments until I can arrange for the car. Would you like to wait outside?"

Martell bowed and made a grateful escape from the heretical chapel. Passing through the building, he emerged into the yard, a cleared space some fifty feet square bordered by scaly, grayish-green shrubbery whose thick-petaled black flowers had an oddly carnivorous look. Four Venusian boys, including Martell's rescuer, were at work on an excavation. They were using manual tools—shovels and picks—which gave Martell the uncomfortable sensation of having slid back into the nineteenth century. Earth's gaudy array of gadgetry, so conspicuous and so familiar, could not be found here.

The boys glared coldly at him and went on with their work. Martell watched. They were lean and supple, and he guessed that their ages ranged from about nine to fourteen, though it was hard to tell. They looked enough alike to be brothers. Their movements were graceful, almost elegant, and their bluish skins gleamed lightly with perspiration. It seemed to Martell that the bony structure of their bodies was even more alien than he had thought; they did improbable things with their joints as they worked.

Abruptly, they tossed their picks and shovels aside and joined hands. The bright eyes closed a moment. Martell saw the loose dirt rise from the excavation pit and collect itself in a neat mound some twenty feet behind it.

They're pushers, Martell thought in wonder. *Look at them!*

Brother Mondschein appeared at that precise moment. "The car is waiting, Brother," he said smoothly.

four

As he entered the Venusian city, Martell could not take his mind from the casual feat of the four boys. They had scooped a few hundred pounds of loose soil from a pit, using esp abilities, and had smugly deposited it just where they wanted it to go.

Pushers! Martell trembled with barely suppressed excitement. The espers of Earth were a numerous tribe now, but their talents were mainly telepathic, not extending in the direction of telekinesis to any significant degree. Nor could the development of the powers be controlled. A program of scheduled breeding, now in its fourth or fifth generation, was intensifying the existing esp powers. It was possible for a gifted esper to reach into a man's mind and rearrange its contents, or to probe for the deepest secrets. There were a few precogs, too, who ranged up and down the time sequence as though all points along it were one point, but they usually burned out in adolescence, and their genes were lost to the pool. Pushers—teleports—who could move physical objects from place to place were as rare as phoenixes on Earth. And here were four of them in a Harmonist chapel's back yard on Venus!

New tensions quivered in Martell. He had made two unexpected discoveries on his first day: the presence of Harmonists on Venus, and the presence of pushers among the Harmonists. His mission had taken on devastating new urgency, suddenly. It was no longer merely a matter of gaining a foothold in an unfriendly world. It was a matter of being outstripped and surpassed by a heresy thought to be in decline.

The car Mondschein had provided dropped Martell off at the Martian Embassy, a blocky little building fronting on the wide plaza that seemed to be the entire town. The Martians had been instrumental in getting Martell to Venus in the first place, and a call on the Ambassador was of priority importance.

The Martians breathed Earth-type air, and they did not care to adapt themselves to Venusian conditions. Once he entered the building, therefore, Martell had to accept a breathing-hood that would protect him against the atmosphere of the planet of his birth.

The Ambassador, Freeman Nat Weiner, was about twice Martell's age, perhaps even older—close to ninety, even. His frame was powerful, with shoulders so wide they seemed out of proportion to his hips and legs.

Weiner said, "So you're here. I really thought you had more sense."

"We're determined people, Freeman Weiner."

"So I know. I've been studying your ways for a long time." Weiner's eyes became remote. "More than sixty years, in fact. I knew your Coordinator Kirby before his conversion—did he ever tell you that?"

"He didn't mention it," Martell said. His flesh crept. Kirby had joined the Vorster Brotherhood about twenty years before Martell had been born. To live a century was nothing unusual these days, and Vorst himself was surely into his twelfth or thirteenth decade, but it was chilling all the same to think of such a span of years.

Weiner smiled. "I came to Earth to negotiate a trade deal, and Kirby was my chaperon. He was with the U.N. then. I gave him a hard time. I was a drinker then. Somehow I don't think he'll ever forget that night." His gaze riveted on Martell's unblinking eyes. "I want you to know, Brother, that I can't provide any protection for you if you're attacked. My responsibility extends only to Martian nationals."

"I understand."

"My advice is the same as it's been from the start. Go back to Earth and live to a ripe old age."

"I can't do that, Freeman Weiner. I've come with a mission to accomplish."

"Ah, dedication! Wonderful! Where will you build your chapel?"

"On the road leading to town. Perhaps closer to town than the Harmonist place."

"And where will you stay until it's built?"

"I'll sleep in the open."

"There's a bird here," Weiner said. "They call it a shrike. It's as big as a dog, and its wings look like old leather, and it has a beak like a spear. I once saw it dive from five hundred feet at a man taking a nap in an open field. The beak pinned him to the ground."

Unperturbed, Martell said, "I survived an encounter with a Wheel today. Perhaps I can dodge a shrike, too. I don't intend to be frightened away."

Weiner nodded. "I wish you luck," he said.

Luck was about all Martell was going to get from the Ambassador, but he was grateful even for that. The Martians were cool toward Earth and all it produced, including its religions. They did not actually hate Earthmen, as the Venusians of both castes appeared to do; the Martians were still Earth-like themselves, and not changed creatures whose bond with the mother world was tenuous at best. But the Martians were tough, aggressive frontiersmen who looked out only for themselves. They served as go-betweens for Earth and Venus because there was profit in it; they accepted missionaries from Earth because there was no harm in it. They were tolerant, in their way, but aloof.

Martell left the Martian Embassy and set about his tasks. He had money and he had energy. He could not hire Venusian labor directly, because it would be an act of pollution for a Venusian even of the low caste to work for an Earthman, but it was possible to commission workmen through Weiner. The Martians, naturally, received a fee for serving as agents.

Workmen were hired and a modest chapel was erected. Martell set up his pocket-size reactor and readied it for use. Alone in the chapel, he stood in silence as the Blue Fire flickered into glowing life.

Martell had not lost his capacity for awe. He was a worldly man, no mystic, yet the sight of the radiation streaming from the water-shielded reactor worked its magic on him, and he dropped to his knees, touching his forehead in the gesture of submission. He could not carry his religious feeling to the stage of idolatry, as the Harmonists did, but he was not without a sense of the might of the movement to which he had pledged his life.

The first day Martell simply carried out the ceremonies of dedication. On the second and third and fourth he waited hopefully for some low-caster who might be curious enough to enter the chapel. None came.

Martell did not care to seek worshipers, not just yet. He preferred that his converts be voluntary, if possible. The chapel remained empty. On the fifth day it was entered—but only by a frog-like creature ten inches long, armed with wicked little horns on its forehead and delicate, deadly-looking spines that sprouted from its shoulders. Were there no life-forms on this planet that went without armor or weaponry, Martell wondered? He shooed the frog out. It growled at him and lunged at his foot with its horns. Martell drew his foot back barely in time, interposing a chair. The frog stabbed at the wood, sank inch-deep with the left horn; when it withdrew, an iridescent fluid trickled down the leg of the chair, burning a pathway through the wood. Martell had never been attacked by a frog before. On the second try he got the animal out the door without suffering harm. A pretty planet, he thought.

The next day came a more cheering visitor: the boy Elwhit. Martell recognized him as one of the boys who had been teleporting dirt behind the Harmonist place. He appeared from nowhere and said to Martell, "You've got Trouble Fungus out there."

"Is that bad?"

"It kills people. Eats them. Don't step in it. Are you really a religious?"

"I like to think so."

"Brother Christopher says you shouldn't be trusted, that you're a heretic. What's a heretic?"

"A heretic is a man who disagrees with another man's religion," Martell said. "I happen to think Brother Christopher's the heretic, as a matter of fact. Would you like to come inside?"

The boy was wide-eyed, endlessly curious, restless. Martell longed to question him about his apparent telekinetic powers, but he knew it was more important at the moment to snare him as a convert. Questions at this point might only frighten him away. Patiently, elaborately, Martell explained what the Vorsters had to offer. It was hard to gauge the boy's reaction. Did abstract concepts mean anything to a ten-year-old? Martell gave him Vorst's book, the simple text. The boy promised to come back.

"Watch out for the Trouble Fungus," he said as he left.

A few days passed. Then the boy returned, with the news that Mondschein had confiscated his book. Martell was pleased at that, in a way. It was a sign of panic among the Harmonists. Let them turn Vorster teachings into something forbidden, and he'd win all of Mondschein's four thousand converts away.

Two days after Elwhit's second visit, Martell had a different caller—a broad-faced man in Harmonist robes. Without introducing himself, he said, "You're trying to steal that boy, Martell. Don't do it."

"He came of his own free will. You can tell Mondschein—"

"The child has curiosity. But he's the one who'll suffer if you keep allowing him to come here. Turn him away the next time, Martell. For his own sake."

"I'm trying to take him away from you for his own sake," the Vorster replied quietly. "And any others who'll come to me. I'm ready to battle with you to have him."

"You'll destroy him," said the Harmonist. "He'll be

pulled apart in the struggle. Let him be. Turn him away."

Martell did not intend to yield. Elwhit was his opening wedge into Venus, and it would be madness to turn him away.

Later that same day there came another visitor, no friendlier than the horned frog. He was a burly Venusian of the lower caste, with armpit-daggers bristling on both sides of his chest. He had not come to worship. He pointed to the reactor and said, "Shut that thing off and dispose of the fissionables within ten hours."

Martell frowned. "It's necessary to our religious observance."

"It's fissionables. Not allowed to run a private reactor here."

"There was no objection at customs," Martell pointed out. "I declared the cobalt-60 for what it was and explained the purpose. It was allowed through."

"Customs is customs. You're in town now, and I say no fissionables. You need a permit to do what you're doing."

"Where do I get a permit?" asked Martell mildly.

"From the police. I'm the police. Request denied. Shut that thing off."

"And if I don't?"

For an instant Martell thought the self-styled policeman would stab him on the spot. The man drew back as though Martell had spat in his face. After an ugly silence he said, "Is that a challenge?"

"It's a question."

"I ask you on my authority to get rid of that reactor. If you defy my authority, you're challenging me. Clear? You don't look like a fighting man. Be smart and do as I say. Ten hours. You hear?"

He went out.

Martell shook his head sadly. Law enforcement a matter of personal pride? Well, it was only to be expected. More to the point: they wanted his reactor off, and without the reactor his chapel would not be a chapel. Could he appeal? To whom? If he dueled with the intruder and slew him, would that give him the right to run the reactor? He could hardly take such a step, anyway.

Martell decided not to give up without a struggle. He sought the authorities, or what passed for authorities here, and after spending four hours waiting to be admitted to the office of a minor official, he was told clearly and coldly to dismantle his reactor at once. His protests were dismissed.

Weiner was no help, either. "Shut the reactor down," the Martian advised.

"I can't function without it," said Martell. "Where'd they get this law about private operation of reactors?"

"They probably invented it to take care of you," Weiner suggested amiably. "There's no help for it, Brother. You'll have to shut down."

Martell returned to the chapel. He found Elwhit waiting on the steps. The boy looked disturbed.

"Don't close," he said.

"I won't." Martell beckoned him inside. "Help me, Elwhit. Teach me. I need to know."

"What?"

"How do you move things around with your mind?"

"I reach into them," the boy said. "I catch hold of what's inside. There's a strength. It's hard to say."

"Is it something you were taught to do?"

"It's like walking. What makes your legs move? What makes them stand up underneath you?"

Martell simmered with frustration. "Can you tell me what it feels like when you do it?"

"Warm. On top of my head. I don't know. I don't feel much. Tell me about the electron, Brother Nicholas. Sing the song of photons to me."

"In a moment," Martell said. He crouched down to get on the boy's eye level. "Can your mother and father move things?"

"A little. I can move them more."

"When did you find out you could do it?"

"The first time I did it."

"And you don't know how you—" Martell paused. What was the use? Could a ten-year-old boy find words to describe a telekinetic function? He did it, as naturally as he breathed. The thing to do was to ship him to Earth, to Santa Fe, and let the Noel Vorst Center for the Biological Sciences have a look at him. Obviously, that was impossible. The boy would never go, and it would hardly be proper to spirit him away.

"Sing me the song," Elwhit prodded.

"In the strength of the spectrum, the quantum, and the holy angstrom—"

The chapel door flew open and three Venusians entered: the police chief and two deputies. The boy pivoted instantly and skittered past them, out the back way.

"Get him!" the police chief roared.

Martell shouted a protest. It was useless. The two deputies pounded after the boy, into the yard. Martell and the police chief followed.

The deputies closed in on the boy. Abruptly, the meatier one was flipping through the air, legs kicking violently as he headed for the deadly patch of Trouble Fungus in the underbrush. He landed hard. There was a muffled groan. Trouble Fungus, Martell had learned by watching it, moved quickly. The carnivorous mold would devour anything organic; its sticky filaments, triggering with awesome speed, went to work instantly. The deputy was trapped in a network of loops whose adhesive enzymes immediately began to operate. Struggling only made it worse. The man thrashed and tugged, but the loops multiplied, stapling him to the ground. And now the digestive enzymes were coming into play. A sweet, sickly odor rose from the Trouble Fungus clump.

Martell had no time to study the process of dissolution. The man caught in his fatal collars of slime was close to death, and the surviving deputy, his face almost black with fear and rage, had drawn a knife on the boy.

Elwhit knocked it out of his hand. He tried to gather strength for another cast into the fungus patch, but his face was sweat-speckled, and bunching muscles in his cheeks told of the inward struggle. The deputy rocked and swayed, resisting the telekinesis. Martell stood frozen. The police chief bounded forward, knife on high.

"Elwhit!" Martell screamed.

Even a telekinetic has no way of defending himself against a stab in the back. The blade went deep. The boy dropped. In the same moment, with the pressure withdrawn, the deputy slipped and fell on his face. The chief seized the wounded, convulsing boy and hurled him into the Trouble Fungus. He landed beside the soft mass of the dead deputy, and Martell watched in horror as the sinister loops locked into place. Sickness assailed him. He ran halfway through the disciplinary techniques before his mind would work properly again.

By then the police chief and his deputy had recovered their calmness. With scarcely a look at the two dissolving corpses, they seized Martell and hauled him back into the chapel.

"You killed a boy," Martell said, breaking loose. "Stabbed him in the back. Where's your honor?"

"I'll settle that before our court, priest. The boy was a murderer. And under the spell of dangerous doctrines. He knew we were closing you down. It was a violation to be here. Why isn't that reactor off?"

Martell groped for words. He wanted to say that he did not intend to accept defeat, that he was staying on here, determined to fight even to the point of martyrdom, despite their order that he shut up shop. But the brutal killing of his only convert had smashed his will.

"I'll shut the reactor down," he said hollowly.

"Go and do it."

Martell dismantled it. They waited, exchanging pleased glances when the light flickered out. The deputy said, "It isn't a real chapel without the light burning, is it, priest?"

"No," Martell replied. "I'm closing the chapel, too, I guess."

"Didn't last long."

"No."

The chief said, "Look at him with his gills flapping. All tricked out to look like one of us, and who's he fooling? We'll teach him."

They moved in on him. They were burly, powerful

men. Martell was unarmed, but he had no fear of them. He could defend himself. They neared him, two nightmare figures, grotesquely inhuman, their eyes bright and slitted, inner lids sliding tensely up and down, small nostrils flickering, gills atremble. Martell had to force himself to remember that he was a monster as much as they; he was a changed one now. Their brother.

"Let's give him a farewell party," the deputy said.

"You've made your point," said Martell. "I'm closing the chapel. Do you need to attack me, too? What are you afraid of? Are ideas that dangerous to you?"

A fist crashed into the pit of his stomach. Martell swayed, caught his breath, forced himself to remain cool. The edge of a hand chopped at his throat. Martell slapped at it, deflected it, and seized the wrist. There was a momentary exchange of ions and the deputy fell back, cursing.

"Look out! He's electric!"

"I mean no harm," said Martell mildly. "Let me go in peace."

Hands went to daggers. Martell waited. Then, slowly, the tension ebbed. The Venusians moved away, apparently willing to let the matter end here. They had, after all, succeeded in throttling the Vorster mission, and now they appeared to have qualms about dealing with the defeated missionary.

"Get yourself out of town, Earthman," the police chief grumbled. "Go where you belong. Don't come mucking around here with your phony religion. We aren't buying any. Go!"

five

There was no blackness quite like the black of the night sky of Venus, Martell thought. It was like a layer of wool swathing the vault of the heavens. Not a hint of a star, not a flicker of a moonbeam cut through that arch of darkness overhead. Yet there was light, occasional and intermittent: great predatory birds, hellishly luminous, skewered the darkness at unpredictable moments. Standing on the rear veranda of the Harmonist chapel, Martell watched a glowing creature soar past, no higher than a hundred feet up, near enough for Martell to see the row of hooked claws that studded the leading edges of the curved, back-swept wings.

"Our birds have teeth as well," said Christopher Mondschein.

"And the frogs have horns," Martell remarked. "Why is this planet so vicious?"

Mondschein chuckled. "Ask Darwin, my friend. It just happened that way. You've met our frogs, then? Deadly little beasts. And you've seen a Wheel. We have amusing fish, too. And carnivorous fauna. But we are without insects. Can you imagine that? No land arthropods at all. Of course, there are some delightful ones in the sea—a kind of scorpion bigger than a man, a sort of lobster with disturbingly large claws—but no one goes into the sea here."

"I understand why," Martell said. Another luminescent bird swooped down, skimmed the trees, and rocketed

124

away. From its flat head jutted a glowing fleshy organ the size of a melon, wobbling on a thick stem.

Mondschein said, "You wish to join us, after all?"

"That's right."

"Infiltrating, Martell? Spying?"

Color came to Martell's cheeks. The surgeons had left him with the flush reaction, although he turned a dull gray when affected now. "Why do you accuse me?" he asked.

"Why else would you want to join us? You were haughty about it last week."

"That was last week. My chapel is closed. I saw a boy who trusted me killed before my eyes. I have no wish to see more such murders."

"So you admit that you were guilty in his death?"

"I admit that I allowed him to jeopardize his life," Martell said.

"We warned you of it."

"But I had no idea of the cruelty of the forces that would strike at me. Now I do. I can't stand alone. Let me join you, Mondschein."

"Too transparent, Martell. You came here bristling with the urge to be a martyr. You gave up too soon. Obviously you want to spy on our movement. Conversions are never that simple, and you're not an easily swayed man. I suspect you, Brother."

"Are you esping me?"

"Me? I don't have a shred of ability. Not a shred. But I have common sense. I know a bit about spying, too. You're here to sniff."

Martell studied a gleaming bird high against the dark backdrop. "You refuse to accept me, then?"

"You can have shelter for the night. In the morning you'll have to go. Sorry, Martell."

No amount of persuasion would alter the Harmonist's decision. Martell was not surprised, nor greatly distressed; joining the Harmonists had been a strategy of doubtful success, and he had more than half expected Mondschein to reject him. Perhaps if he had waited six months before applying, the response would have been different.

He remained aloof while the little group of Harmonists performed evening vespers. They were not called "vespers," of course, but Martell could not avoid identifying the heretics with the older religion. Three altered Earthmen were stationed at the mission, and the voices of the two subordinates joined with Mondschein's in hymns that seemed offensive in their religiosity and yet faintly moving at the same time. Seven low-caste Venusians took part in the service. Afterward Martell shared a dinner of unknown meat and acrid wine with the three Harmonists. They seemed comfortable enough in his presence, almost smug. One, Bradlaugh, was slim and fragile-looking, with elongated arms and comically blunt features. The other, Lazarus, was robust and athletic, his eyes oddly blank, his skin stretched mask-tight over his broad face. He was the one who had visited Martell's ill-fated chapel. Martell suspected that Lazarus was an esper. His last name aroused the missionary's curiosity.

"Are you related to *the* Lazarus?" Martell asked.

"His grandnephew. I never knew the man."

"No one seems to have known him," said Martell. "It often occurs to me that the esteemed founder of your heresy may have been a myth."

Faces stiffened around the table. Mondschein said, "I met someone who knew him once. An impressive man, they say he was: tall and commanding, with an air of majesty."

"Like Vorst," Martell said.

"Very much like Vorst. Natural leaders, both of them," said Mondschein. He rose. "Brothers, good night."

Martell was left alone with Bradlaugh and Lazarus. An uncomfortable silence followed; after a while Bradlaugh rose and said coolly, "I'll show you to your room."

The room was small, with a simple cot. Martell was content. Fewer religious symbols decorated the room than there might have been, and it was a place to sleep. He took care of his devotions quickly and closed his eyes. After a while sleep came—a thin crust of slumber over an abyss of turmoil.

The crust was pierced.

There came the sound of laughter, booming and harsh. Something thumped against the chapel walls. Martell struggled to wakefulness in time to hear a thick voice cry, "Give us the Vorster!"

He sat up. Someone entered his room: Mondschein, he realized. "They're drunk," the Harmonist whispered. "They've been roistering all over the countryside all night, and now they're here to make trouble."

"The Vorster!" came a roar from outside.

Martell peered through his window. At first he saw nothing; then, by the gleam of the light-cells studding the chapel's outer walls, he picked out seven or eight titanic figures, striding unsteadily back and forth in the courtyard.

"High-casters!" Martell gasped.

"One of our espers brought the word an hour ago," said Mondschein. "It was bound to happen sooner or later. I'll go out and calm them."

"They'll kill you."

"It's not me they're after," said Mondschein, and left.

Martell saw him emerge from the building. He was dwarfed by the ring of drunken Venusians, and from the way they closed in on him, Martell was certain that they would do him some harm. But they hesitated. Mondschein faced them squarely. At this distance Martell could not hear what they were saying. A parley of some sort, perhaps. The big men were armed and reeling. Some glowing creature shot past the knot of figures, giving Martell a sudden glimpse of the faces of the high-caste men: alien, distorted, terrifying. Their cheekbones were like knifeblades; their eyes mere slits. Mondschein, his back to the window now, was gesticulating, no doubt talking rapidly and earnestly.

One of the Venusians scooped up a twenty-pound boulder and lobbed it against the mission's whitewashed wall. Martell nibbled a knuckle. Fragments of conversation came to him, ugly words: "Let us have him. . . . We could take you all. . . . Time we crushed all you toads. . . ."

Mondschein's hands were upraised now. Imploringly, Martell wondered, or was he simply trying to keep the Venusians at bay? Martell thought of praying. But it seemed a hollow, futile gesture. One did not pray for direct reward, in the Brotherhood. One lived well and served the cause, and reward came. Martell felt tranquil. He slipped into his robe and went outside.

Never before had he been this close to a group of high-casters. There was a rank odor about them, an odor that reminded Martell of the scent of the Wheel. They stared in disbelief as the Vorster emerged.

"What do they want?" Martell asked.

Mondschein gaped at him. "Go back inside! I'm negotiating with them!"

One of the Venusians unfurled a sword. He drove it a foot into the spongy earth, leaned on it, and said, "There's the priestling now! What are we waiting for?"

Mondschein said helplessly to Martell, "You shouldn't have come out. There might have been a chance to quiet them down."

"Not a chance. They'll destroy your whole mission here if I don't pacify them. I've got no right to bring that on you."

"You're our guest," Mondschein reminded him.

Martell did not care to accept the charity of heretics. He had come to the Harmonists, as they had guessed, in the hope of spying; that had failed, as had the rest of his mission here, and he would not hide behind Mondschein's green robe. He caught the older man's arm and said, "Go inside. Fast!"

Mondschein shrugged and disappeared. Martell swung around to face the Venusians.

"Why are you here?" he asked.

A gob of spittle caught him in the face. Without speaking directly to him, one Venusian said, "We'll skewer him and throw him in Ludlow Pond, eh?"

"Hack him! Spit him!"

"Stake him out for a Wheel!"

Martell said, "I came here in peace. I bring you the gift of life. Why won't you listen? What are you afraid of?"

They were big children, he saw, reveling in their power to crush an ant. "Let's all sit down by that tree. Allow me to talk to you for a while. I'll take the drunkenness out of you. If you'll only give me your hand—"

"Watch out!" a Venusian roared. "He stings!"

Martell reached for the nearest of the giants. The man leaped back with a most ungallant display of edginess. An instant later, as though to atone for bolting that way, his sword was out, a glittering anachronism nearly as long as Martell himself. Two Venusians drew their daggers. They strutted forward, and Martell filled his altered lungs with alien air and waited for the shedding of his no-longer-red blood, and then suddenly he was no longer there.

"How did you get here?" Ambassador Nat Weiner asked.

"I wish I knew," said Martell.

The sudden brightness of the Martian's office stabbed at Martell's eyes. He still could see the descending blades of the fearsome swords, and he was rocked by a sensation of unreality, as though he had left one dream to enter another in which he was dreaming yet a different thread.

"This is a maximum-security building," said Weiner. "You have no right to be here."

"I have no right even to be alive," replied the missionary flatly.

six

Broodingly, Martell considered retreating to Earth to tell Santa Fe what he knew. He could go to the Vorst Center, where, less than a year ago, he had gone into a room as an Earthman, to be turned by whirling knives and lashing lasers into an alien thing. He could request an interview with Reynolds Kirby and let that grizzled, thin-lipped centenarian know that the Venusians had telekinesis, that they could deflect a Wheel or throw an attacker into Trouble Fungus or speed a living human figure safely across five miles and pass him through walls.

Santa Fe would have to know. The situation looked bad. Harmonists snugly established on Venus, and the place chock-full of teleports—it could mean a disastrous blow to Vorst's master plan. Of course, the Vorsters on Earth had made great gains, too. They were masters of the planet. Their laboratories had run simulated life spans that showed a tally of from three to four hundred years, without organ replacement—simple regeneration from within, amounting to a kind of immortality. But immortality was only one Vorster goal. The other was transport to the unreachable stars.

And there the Harmonists had their big lead. They had teleports who already could work miracles. Given a few generations of genetic work, they might be sending expeditions to other solar systems. Once you could move a man five miles in safety, it was only a quantitative jump, not qualitative, to get him to Procyon. Martell had to tell them. Santa Fe called to him—that vast sprawl of buildings where technicians split genes and laboriously pasted them back together, where esper families submitted to an endless round of tests, where bionics men performed wonders beyond comprehension.

But he did not go. A personal report seemed unnecessary. A message cube would do just as well. Earth now was an alien world to Martell, and he was uneasy about returning to it, living in breathing-suits. He balked at making the return journey.

Through the good offices of Nat Weiner, Martell recorded a cube and had it shipped to Kirby at Santa Fe. He remained at the Martian Embassy while waiting for his reply. He had set forth the situation on Venus as he understood it, expressing his great fear that the Harmonists were too far ahead and would have the stars. In time Kirby's reply arrived. He thanked Martell for his invaluable data. And he expressed a calming note: the Harmonists, he said, were men. If they were to reach the stars, it would be a human achievement. Not theirs, not ours, but everyone's, for the way would be opened. Did Brother Martell follow that reasoning, Kirby asked?

Martell felt quicksand beneath him. What was Kirby saying? Means and ends were hopelessly jumbled. Was the purpose of the order fulfilled if heretics conquered the universe? In distress, he stood before the improvised altar in the room Weiner had given him, seeking answers to unaskable questions.

A few days later he returned to the Harmonists.

seven

Martell stood with Christopher Mondschein by the edge of a sparkling lake. Through the clouds came the dull glow of the masked sun, imparting a faint gleam to the water-that-was-not-water. It was not that trickle of sunlight that made the water sparkle, though; it teemed with luminous coelenterates that lined its shallow bottom. Their tentacles, waving in the currents, emitted a gentle greenish radiance.

There were other creatures in the lake, too. Martell saw them gliding beneath the surface, ribbed and bony, with gnashing jaws and metallic fins. Now and then a snout split the water and a slim, ugly creature whipped twenty yards through the air before subsiding. From the depths came writhing, sucker-tipped tendrils that belonged to monsters Martell did not care to know.

Mondschein said, "I thought I'd never see you again."

"When I went out to face the Venusians?"

"No. Afterward, when you holed up with the Martians. I thought you were making arrangements to go back to Earth. You know it's hopeless to try to plant a Vorster chapel here."

"I know," Martell said. "But I've got that boy's death on my conscience. I can't leave. I lured him into visiting me, and he died for it. He'd be alive if I had turned him away. And I'd be dead if you hadn't had one of your other little Venusians teleport me to safety."

"Elwhit was one of our finest prospects," Mondschein said sadly. "But he had this streak of wildness—the thing

132

that brought him to us in the first place. A restless boy, he was. I wish you had left him alone."

"I did what I had to do," Martell replied. "I'm sorry it worked out so awfully." He followed the path of a sinuous black serpent that swept from right to left across the lake. It extended telescoping arms in a sudden terrifying gesture and enveloped a low-flying bird. Martell said carefully, "I didn't come back here to spy on you. I came back to join your order."

Mondschein's domed blue forehead wrinkled a little. "Please. We've been through all this already."

"Test me! Have one of your espers read me! I swear it, Mondschein. I'm sincere."

"They've embedded a pack of hypnotic commands in you in Santa Fe. I know. I've been through it myself. They sent you here to be a spy, but you don't know it yourself, and if we probed you, we might have trouble finding out the truth. You'll soak up all you can about us, and then you'll return to Santa Fe, and they'll toss you to a debriefing esper who'll pump it all out of you. Eh?"

"No. Not at all."

"Are you sure?"

"Listen," said Martell, "I don't think they did anything to my mind in Santa Fe. I came to you because I belong on Venus. I've been changed." He held out his hands. "My skin is blue. My metabolism is a biologist's nightmare. I've got gills. I'm a Venusian, and this is where the changed ones go. But I can't be a Vorster here, because the natives won't have it. Therefore I've got to join you. Do you see?"

Mondschein nodded. "I still think you're a spy."

"I tell you—"

"Stay calm," said the Harmonist. "*Be* a spy. That's quite all right. You can stay. You can join us. You'll be our bridge, Brother. You'll be the link that will span the Vorsters and the Harmonists. Play both sides if you like. That's exactly what we want."

Once again Martell felt the foundations giving way beneath his feet. He imagined himself in a dropshaft with the gravity field suddenly gone—falling, falling, endlessly falling. He peered into the mild eyes of the older man and perceived that Mondschein must be in the grip of some crazy ecumenical scheme, some private fantasy that—

He said, "Are you trying to put the orders back together?"

"Not personally. It's part of the plan of Lazarus."

Martell thought Mondschein was referring to his own assistant. He said, "Is he in charge here or are you?"

Smiling, Mondschein replied, "I don't mean my Lazarus here. I mean David Lazarus, the founder of our order."

"He's dead."

"Certainly. But we still follow the course he mapped for us half a century ago. And that course envisages the eventual reuniting of the orders. It has to come, Martell. We each have something the other wants. You have Earth and immortality. We have Venus and teleportation. There's bound to be a pooling of interests, and possibly you'll be one of the men who'll help to bring it about."

"You aren't serious!"

"As serious as I know how to be," said Mondschein. Martell saw the darkening of his expression; the amiable mask dropped away. "Do you want to live forever, Martell?"

"I'm not eager to die. Except for some overriding purpose, of course."

"The translation is that you want to live as long as you can, with honor."

"Right."

"The Vorsters are getting nearer to that goal every day. We have some idea of what's going on in Santa Fe. Once, about forty years ago, we stole the contents of an entire longevity lab. It helped us, but not enough. We didn't have the substratum of knowledge. On the other hand, we've made some strides, too, as I think you've discovered. Will it be worth a reunion, do you think? We'll have the stars—you'll have eternity. Stay here and spy, Brother. I think—and I know Lazarus thought—that the fewer secrets we have, the faster our progress will be."

Martell did not reply. A boy emerged from the woods—

a Venusian boy, possibly the one who had saved him from the Wheel, perhaps the dead Elwhit's brother. They looked so interchangeable in their strangeness. Instantly Mondschein's manner changed. He donned a bland smile; cosmic matters receded.

"Bring us a fish," he told the boy.

"Yes, Brother Christopher."

There was silence. Veins throbbed on the boy's forehead. In the center of the lake the water boiled, white foam splashing upward. A creature appeared, scaly and dull gold in color. It hovered in the air, ten feet of frustrated fury, its great underslung jaw opening and closing impotently. The beast soared toward the group on the shore.

"Not that one!" Mondschein gasped.

The boy laughed. The huge fish slipped back into the lake. An instant later something opalescent throbbed on the ground at Martell's feet—a toothy, snapping thing a foot and a half long, with fins that nearly were legs, and a fan-like tail in which wicked spikes stirred and quivered. Martell leaped away, but he was in no danger, he realized. The fish's skull caved in as though smitten by an invisible fist, and it lay still. Martell knew terror in that moment. The slender, laughing boy, who had so mischievously pulled that monster from the waters and then this equally deadly little thing, could kill with a flicker of his frontal lobes.

Martell stared at Mondschein. "Your pushers—are they all Venusians?"

"All."

"I hope you can keep them under control."

"I hope so, too," Mondschein replied. He seized the dead fish carefully by a stubby fin, holding it so the tail-spikes pointed away from him. "A great delicacy," he said. "Once we remove the poison sacs, of course. We'll catch two or three more and have a devilfish dinner tonight to celebrate your conversion, Brother Martell."

eight

⸻⸻⸻⸻

They gave him a room, and they gave him menial jobs to do, and in their spare time they instructed him in the tenets of Transcendent Harmony. Martell found the room sufficient and the labor unobjectionable, but it was a more difficult matter to swallow the theology. He could not pretend, to himself or to them, that it had any meaning for him. Warmed-over Christianity, a dollop of Islam, a tinge of latter-day Buddhism—all spread over a structure borrowed shamelessly from Vorst—it was an unpalatable mixture for Martell. There was syncretism enough in the Vorster teachings, but Martell accepted those because he had been born to them. Schooling himself in heresy was a different matter.

They began with Vorst, accepting him as a prophet just as Christianity respected Moses and Islam honored Jesus. But, of course, there was the later dispensation, represented by the figure of David Lazarus. Vorster writings made no mention of Lazarus. Martell knew of him only from his studies in the history of the Brotherhood of the Immanent Radiance, which mentioned Lazarus in passing as a tangential figure, an early supporter of Vorst's and then an early dissenter.

But Vorst lived, and, so said both groups, he would live forever, in tune with the cosmos, the First Immortal. Lazarus was dead, a martyr to honesty, cruelly betrayed and slain by the domineering Vorsters in their moment of triumph on Earth.

The Book of Lazarus told the sad story. Martell twitched beneath his skin as he read it:

Lazarus was trusting and without guile. But the men whose hearts were hard came upon him and slew him in the night, and fed his body to the converter so that not even a molecule remained. And when Vorst learned of their deed, he wept and said, "I wish you had slain me instead, for now you have given him an immortality he can never lose. . . ."

Martell could find nothing in the Harmonist scriptures that was actually discreditable to Vorst. Even the assassination of Lazarus itself clearly was shown to be the work of underlings, carried out without Vorst's knowledge or desire. And through the writings ran an expression of hope that one day the faith would be reunited, though it was stressed that the Harmonists must submit to unity only out of a position of strength, and in complete equality.

A few months before, Martell would have regarded their pretensions as absurd. On Earth they were a pipsqueak movement, losing members from year to year. Now, among them if not entirely of them, he saw that he had badly underestimated their power. Venus was theirs. The high-caste natives might boast and swagger, but they were no longer the masters. There were espers among the downtrodden lower-caste Venusians—pushers, no less—and they had given their destinies into Harmonist hands.

Martell worked. He learned. He listened. And he feared.

The stormy season came. From the eternal clouds there burst tongues of lightning that set all Venus ablaze. Torrents of bitter rain flailed the flat plains. Trees five hundred feet tall were ripped from the ground and hurled great distances. From time to time, high-casters arrived at the chapel to sneer or to threaten, and in the shrieking gales they roared their blustering defiance, while within the building grinning low-caste boys waited to defend their teachers if necessary. Once Martell saw three high-caste men thrown twenty yards back from the entrance as they tried to break in. "A stroke of lightning," they told one another. "We're lucky to be alive."

In the spring came warmth. Stripping to his alien skin, Martell worked in the fields, Bradlaugh and Lazarus beside him. He did not yet teach at all. He was well versed by now in the Harmonist teachings, but it was all from the outside in, and a seemingly impermeable barrier of skepticism prevented it from getting deeper.

Then, on a steamy day when sweat rolled in rivers from the altered pores of the four former Earthmen at the Harmonist chapel, Brother Leon Bradlaugh joined the blessed company of martyrs. It happened swiftly. They were in the fields, and a shadow crossed above them, and a silent voice within Martell screamed, "Watch out!"

He could not move. But this was not his day to die. Something plummeted from the sky, something heavy and leather-winged, and Martell saw a beak a yard long plunge into Bradlaugh's chest, and there was the fountaining of coppery blood. Bradlaugh lay outstretched with the shrike on him, and the great beak was withdrawn, and Martell heard a sound of rending and tearing.

They gave the last rites to what was left of Bradlaugh. Brother Christopher Mondschein presided, and called Martell to his side afterward.

"There are only three of us now," he said. "Will you teach, Brother Martell?"

"I'm not one of you."

"You wear a green tunic. You know our creed. Do you still think of yourself as a Vorster, Brother?"

"I—I don't know what I am," answered Martell. "I need to think about this."

"Give me your answer soon. There's much to be done here, Brother."

Martell did not realize that he would know within a day where he really stood. A day after Bradlaugh's funeral the regular thrice-weekly passenger ship from Mars arrived. Martell knew nothing of it until Mondschein came to him and said, "Take one of the boys in the car, and do it quickly. A man needs saving!"

Martell did not ask questions. Somehow, news had

traveled down a chain of espers, and it was his task simply to obey. He entered the car. One of the little Venusian acolytes slipped in beside him.

"Which way?" Martell asked.

The boy gestured. Martell thumbed the starter. The car sped down the road, toward the airport. When they had gone two and a half miles, the boy grunted a command to halt. The car stopped.

A figure in a blue tunic stood by the side of the road, his back to the bole of a mighty tree. Two suitcases lay open on the highway, and a razor-backed beast with a flattened snout and boar-like tusks was rooting through them, while its mate charged the newly arrived Vorster. The beleaguered man was kicking and lashing at the beast.

The boy hopped from the car. Without sign of strain, he caused the two animals to rise and slam into trees on the far side of the road. They dropped to the ground, looking dazed but determined. The boy levitated them again and struck their heads together. When they fell this time, they swung around and fled into the underbrush.

Martell said, "Venus always seems to welcome new-comers like that. My greeting committee was a thing called a Wheel, which I hope you never meet. I'd be in ribbons now except that a Venusian boy was kind enough to teleport it over on its side. Are you a missionary?"

The man seemed too dazed to reply immediately. He knotted his hands together, released them, adjusted his tunic. Finally he said, "Yes—yes, I am. From Earth."

"Surgically changed, then?"

"That's right."

"So am I. I'm Nicholas Martell. How are things in Santa Fe, Brother?"

The newcomer's lips tightened. He was a fleshless little man, a year or two younger than Martell. He said, "How can that matter to you if you're Martell? Martell the heretic? Martell the renegade?"

"No," Martell said. "That is—I—"

He fell silent. His hands tensely smoothed the fabric of his Harmonist green tunic. His cheeks were burning. He realized painfully the truth about himself—that the change in him had worked inward from without—and suddenly he could not meet the gaze of his altered successor in the Venus mission, and he turned, staring into the thicket of the no longer very alien forest.

FOUR

Lazarus Come Forth
2152

kills people. Hate them. Don't stop in it. Are you

able to think up

Brother Christopher says you shouldn't be trusted,
you're a heretic. What's a heretic?"

one

Mars Monotrack One, the main line, ran from east to west like a girdle of concrete flanking the planet's western hemisphere. To the north lay the Lake District with its fertile fields; to the south, closer to the equator, was the belt of throbbing compressor stations that had done so much to foster the miracle. The discerning eye could still make out the old craters and gouges of the landscape, hidden now under a dusting of sawtooth grass and occasional forests of pine.

The gray concrete pylons of the monotrack marched to the horizon. Spurs carried the line to the settlements of the outlands, and they were always adding new spurs as the new settlements sprouted. Logistically, it might have been simpler to have all the Martians live in One Big City, but the Martians were not that sort of people.

Spur 7Y was being added now, advancing in ungainly bounds toward the new outpost of Beltran Lakes. Already the pylon foundations had gone up three-quarters of the way from Mono One to the settlement; a vast pylon-layer was working its way through the countryside, gobbling up sand from ten yards down and spewing out concrete slabs that it stapled into the ground. Gobble, spew, staple, and move on—gobble, spew, staple. The machine moved rapidly, guided by a neatly homeostatic brain that kept it on course. Behind it came the other machines to lay track between the pylons and string the utility lines that would follow the same route. The Martian settlers had many miracles at their command, but microwave kickover of usable electric power wasn't one of them—not yet—and so the lines had to get strung from place to place even as in the Middle Ages.

The monotrack system was intended for heavy-duty transportation. The Martians used quickboats, like everybody else, for getting themselves from place to place. But the slim little vehicles weren't much use in the shipment of construction materials, and this was a planet under construction. Now that the *re*construction phase was over. The Terraformers were gone. Mars was a bosky dell, here in this year of grace 2152, and now the task was to plant a civilization on the finally hospitable planet. The Martians numbered in the millions. They had passed their frontiersman stage and were settling down to enjoy the pleasures of a good commercial boom. And the monotrack marched on, mile after mile, skirting the seas, rimming the lakes and rivers.

The dogwork was done by clever machines. Men rode herd on the machinery, though. You never could tell when the homeostasis would slip ever so slightly and your pylon-layer would go berserk. It had happened a few years ago, and somehow the cutoff relays had been blanked out of the circuit, and before anyone could do anything there were sixteen miles of pylons crisscrossing Holliman Lake—eight hundred feet under water. Martians hate wastefulness. The machines had shown that they were not entirely trustworthy, and thereafter they were watched.

Watching over the construction of this particular spur of Monotrack One was a lean, sun-bronzed man of sixty-eight named Paul Weiner, who had good political connections, and a plump red-haired man named Hadley Donovan, who did not. Redheads were rare on Mars for the usual statistical reasons; plump men were rare, too, but not so rare as they once had been. Life was softer these days, and so were the younger Martians. Hadley Donovan was amused by the antics of his gun-toting elders, with their formal etiquette, their theatrically taut bodies, their sense of high personal importance. Perhaps it had been necessary to wear those poses in the pioneer days on Mars, Donovan thought, but all that had been over for thirty years. He had allowed himself the luxury of a modest paunch. He knew that Paul Weiner felt contempt for him.

The feeling was mutual.

The two men sat side by side in a landcrawler, edging through the roadless landscape twenty miles ahead of the pylon-laying rig. Transponders bleeped at appropriate intervals; on the control board in front of them, colors came and went in an evanescent flow. Weiner was supposed to be monitoring the doings of the construction rig behind them; Donovan was checking out the planned route of the track, hunting for pockets of subsurface mushiness that the pylon-builder would not be clever enough to evaluate.

Donovan was trying to do both jobs at once. He didn't dare let a political appointee like Weiner have any real responsibility in the work. Weiner was the nephew of Nat Weiner, who stood high in ruling councils, was a hundred-and-some years old, and went to Earth every few years to have the Vorsters pluck out his pancreas or his kidneys or his carotid arteries and implant handy artificial substitutes. Nat Weiner was going to live forever, probably, and he was gradually filling the entire civil service up with members of his family, and Hadley Donovan, trying to oversee a job that really required two men's full attention, felt vague desperation as he scanned his own board and covertly glanced over at Weiner's every thirty seconds or so.

Something was glowing purple on the Anomaly Screen. Donovan wondered about it, but he was too busy with his own part of the job to mention it, and then Weiner was drawling, "I got something peculiar over here, Donovan. What do you make of it, Freeman?"

Donovan kicked the crawler to a halt and studied the board. "Underground rock vault, looks like. Three—four miles off the track."

"Think we ought to take a look?"

"Why bother?" Donovan asked. "The track won't come anywhere near it."

"You aren't curious? Might be a treasure vault left by the Old Martians."

Donovan didn't dignify that with a reply.

"What do you think it is, then?" Weiner asked. "Maybe it's a cave carved by an underground stream. You think so? All that subsurface water Mars had before they Terraformed it? Rivers flowing under the desert?"

Feeling the needles, Donovan said, "It's probably just a crawl-space left by the Terraforming engineers. I don't see why—oh, hell. All right. Let's go investigate. Shut the whole project down for half an hour. What do I care?"

He began throwing switches.

It was a foolish, pointless interruption, but the older man's curiosity had to be satisfied. Treasure cave! Underground stream! Donovan had to admit that he couldn't think of any rational reason why there'd be such a pocket of open space underground here. Geologically, it didn't make much sense.

They cut across to it. It turned out to be about twenty feet down, with undisturbed-looking grass growing above it. Some close-range pinging confirmed that the vault was about ten feet long, a dozen feet wide, eight or nine feet deep. Donovan was convinced that it had been left by the Terraformers. But it wasn't on the charts, at any rate. He summoned a dig-robot and put it to work.

In ten minutes the roof of the vault lay bare: a slab of green fusion-glass. Donovan shivered a little. Weiner said, "I think we got ourselves a grave here, you know?"

"Let's leave it. This isn't our business. We'll report it and—"

"What do we have here?" Weiner asked, and slipped his hand into an opening. He seemed to be caressing something within. Quickly he drew his hand back as a yellow glow spread over the top of the vault.

A voice said, "May the blessing of eternal harmony be on you, friends. You have come to the temporary resting place of Lazarus. Qualified medical assistance will revive me. I ask your help. Please do not attempt to open this vault except with qualified medical assistance."

Silence.

The voice said again, "May the blessing of eternal harmony be on you, friends. You have come to the temporary—"

"A voice-cube," Donovan murmured.

"Look!" Weiner gasped, and pointed to the clearing vault-roof. The glass, lit from below, was transparent now. Donovan peered down into a rectangular vault. A thin, hawk-faced man lay on his back in a nutrient bath, feed-lines connected to his limbs and trunk. It was something like a Nothing Chamber, but far more elaborate. The sleeper wore a smile. Arcane symbols were inscribed on the walls of the chamber. Donovan recognized them as Harmonist symbols. That Venusian cult. He felt a stab of confusion. What had they stumbled on here? "The temporary resting place of Lazarus," the voice-cube said. Lazarus was the prophet of the Harmonists. To Donovan, all of these religions were equally inane. He would have to report this discovery now, and there would be delay in the construction project, and he himself would be pushed unwantedly into prominence, and—

And none of it would ever have happened if Weiner had been dozing off as usual. Why had he noticed the anomaly on the board? Why?

"We better tell somebody about this," Weiner said. "I think it's important."

two

In a small jungle-fringed building on Venus, eight men who were not men faced a ninth. All wore the cyanotic blue skins of Venus, though only three had been born with those skins. The others were surgical products, Earthmen converted to Venusians. Not just their bodies had been converted, either. The six changed ones had all been Vorsters at one time in their spiritual development.

The Vorsters were the most powerful figures on Earth. But this was not Earth but Venus, and Venus was in the hands of the Harmonists, sometimes called the Lazarites after their martyred founder, David Lazarus. Lazarus, the prophet of Transcendent Harmony, had been put to death by Vorster underlings more than sixty years before. Now, to the consternation of his followers—

"Brother Nicholas, may we have your report?" asked Christopher Mondschein, the head of the Harmonists on Venus.

Nicholas Martell, a slender, dogged man in early middle age, stared at his eight colleagues wearily. In the past few days he had had little sleep and many profound jolts to his equilibrium. Martell had made the round trip to Mars to check on the astonishing report that had flashed to the three planets not long before.

He said, "It's exactly as the news story had it. Two workmen coming upon a vault while supervising the construction of a monotrack spur."

"You saw the vault?" asked Mondschein.

"I saw the vault. They've got it cordoned."

"What about Lazarus?"

"There was a figure inside the vault. It matched the image of Lazarus in Rome. It resembled all the portraits. The vault's a sort of Nothing Chamber, and the figure is hooked up inside. The Martian authorities have checked the circuitry of the vault, and they say that it's likely to blow sky-high if anybody tampers with it."

"And the figure," persisted a hollow-cheeked man named Emory. "The figure is Lazarus?"

"Looks like Lazarus," Martell said. "You must remember I never saw Lazarus in the flesh. I wasn't born yet when he died. *If* he died."

"Don't say that," Emory snapped. "This is a hoax. Lazarus died, all right. He was fed to the converter. There's nothing left of him but loose protons and electrons and neutrons."

"So it says in our Scripture," declared Mondschein warily. He closed his eyes a moment. He was the oldest man present; he had been on Venus almost sixty years and had built this branch of the movement to its present dominant position. He said, "There is always the possibility that our text is corrupt."

"No!" The outburst came from Emory, young and conservative. "How can you say that?"

Mondschein shrugged. "The early years of our movement, Brother, are shrouded in doubt. We know there was a Lazarus, that he worked with Vorst at Santa Fe, that he quarreled with Vorst over procedure and was assassinated, or at least put out of the way. But all that was a long time ago. There's no one left in the movement who was directly associated with Lazarus. We aren't as long-lived as the Vorsters, you know. So if it happened that Lazarus wasn't stuffed into a converter, but was simply carried off to Mars in suspended animation and plugged into a Nothing Chamber for sixty or seventy years—"

There was silence in the room. Martell gave Mondschein a sidelong glance of distress. It was Emory who finally said, "What if he's revived and claims to be Lazarus? What happens to the movement?"

Mondschein replied, "We'll face that when we get to it. According to Brother Nicholas, there seems to be some doubt as to whether the vault can be opened at all."

"That's correct," Martell said. "If it's wired to explode when tampered with—"

"Let's hope it is," put in Brother Ward, who had not spoken. "For our purposes, the best Lazarus is a martyred Lazarus. We can keep the tomb as a shrine, and send pilgrimages there, and perhaps get the Martians interested. But if he comes back to life and begins to upset things—"

"What is in that vault *is not Lazarus,*" Emory said.

Mondschein stared at him in amazement. Emory seemed ready to crack apart.

"Perhaps you'd better rest awhile," Mondschein suggested. "You're taking this much too much to heart."

Martell said, "It's a disturbing business, Christopher. If you had seen that figure in the vault—he looks so angelic so confident of resurrection—"

Emory groaned. Mondschein furrowed his brow a moment, and in response the door opened and one of the native Venusians entered, one of the espers the Harmonists had been collecting so long on Venus.

"Brother Emory is tired, Neerol," Mondschein said. The Venusian nodded. His hand closed on Emory's wrist, dark purple against deep indigo. A nexus formed; there was a momentary neural flow; sluices opened somewhere within Emory's brain. Emory relaxed. The Venusian led him from the room.

Mondschein looked around at the others. "We have to operate under the assumption," he said, "that the genuine body of David Lazarus has turned up on Mars, that our book is in error about his fate, and that there's at least the possibility that the body in that vault can be brought to life. The question is, how are we going to react?"

Martell, who had seen the vault and who would never be quite the same, said, "You know I've always been skeptical of the charismatic value of the Lazarus story. But I see this as operating to our advantage. If we can gain possession of the vault and make it the symbolic center of our movement—something to capture the public imagination—"

"Exactly," Ward said. "It's always been our big selling point that we've got a mythos. The competition's got Vorst and his medical miracles, Santa Fe and all that, but nothing to stir the heart. We've had the martyrdom of Lazarus, and it's helped us take control of Venus, which the Vorsters never were able to do. And now, with Lazarus himself come forth from the dead—"

"You miss the point," said Mondschein thinly. "What turned up on Mars doesn't tally with the myth. Lazarus isn't *supposed* to be resurrected in the flesh. He was blasted to atoms. Suppose archaeologists found that Christ had really been beheaded, not crucified? Suppose it came to light that Mohammed never set foot in Mecca? We've been caught with our mythology askew—if this is really Lazarus. It could destroy us. It could wreck all we've built."

three

Thirty miles from the quaint old city of Santa Fe, the sprawling laboratories of the Noel Vorst Center for the Biological Sciences rose within a ring of dark mountains. Here surgeons transformed living creatures into alien flesh. Here technicians laboriously manipulated genes. Here families of espers submitted to an endless round of experiments, and bionics men prodded their subjects mercilessly toward a new realm of existence. The Center was a mighty machine, bristling with purposefulness.

Inconceivably old men were at the heart of the machine.

The core of the movement was the domed building near the main auditorium, where Noel Vorst lived when at Santa Fe. Vorst, the Founder, acknowledged more than a century and a quarter of life. There were those who said that he was dead, that the Vorst who occasionally appeared at the chapels of the Brotherhood was a robot, a simulacrum. Vorst himself found this amusing. More of him was artificial than flesh, at this point, but he was undeniably alive, with no immediate plans for dying. If he had planned to die, he never would have gone to the trouble of founding the Brotherhood of the Immanent Radiance. There had been hard years at first. It is not pleasant to be deemed a crackpot.

Among those who had deemed Vorst a crackpot in those days was his present second-in-command, the Hemispheric Coordinator, Reynolds Kirby. Kirby had stumbled into the Brotherhood at a time of personal stress, looking for something to cling to in a storm. That had been in 2077. He was still clinging, seventy-five years later. By now he was virtually Vorst's alter ego, an adjunct of the Founder's soul.

The Founder had been less than candid with Kirby about this Lazarus enterprise, though. For the first time in many years Vorst had held the details of a project entirely to himself. Some things could not be shared. When they were matters concerning David Lazarus, Vorst held them *in pectore,* unable to take even Kirby into his confidence.

The Founder sat cradled in a webfoam net that spared him most of gravity's pull. Once he had been a vigorous, dynamic giant of a man, and when he had to, he could wear that set of attributes even now, but he preferred comfort. It was necessary to spare his strength. His plan had fulfilled itself well, but he knew that without his guiding presence it might all yet come to nothing.

Kirby sat before him, thin-lipped, grizzled, his body, like Vorst's, a patchwork of artificial organs. The Vorster laboratories no longer needed such clumsy devices to prolong youth. Within the last generation they had managed to stimulate regeneration from within, the body's own rebirth, always the most preferable way. Kirby had come along too early for that; so had Vorst. For them, organ replacement was the road to conditional immortality. With luck, they might last two or three centuries, undergoing periodic overhauls. Younger men, those who had joined the movement in the last forty years, might hope for several hundred years more than that. Some now living, Vorst knew, would never die.

Vorst said, "About this Lazarus thing—"

His voice came from a vocoder box. The larynx had gone sixty years ago. The effect was naturalistic enough, though.

"We can infiltrate our men," Kirby said. "I can work through Nat Weiner. We'll get a bomb clapped onto that vault and give Mr. Lazarus his eternal repose."

"No."

"No?"

"Of course not," Vorst said. He lowered the shutters that lubricated his eyes. "Nothing must happen to that vault or the man who's in it. We'll infiltrate, all right. You'll have to use your pull with Weiner. But not to destroy. We're going to bring Lazarus back to life."

"We're—"

"As a gift to our friends, the Harmonists. To show our enduring affection for our brothers in the Oneness."

"No," Kirby said. Muscles roiled in his fleshless face, and Vorst could see him making adrenal adjustments, trying to stay calm in the face of this assault on his sense of logic. "This is the prophet of the heretics," Kirby said quietly. "I know that you've got your reasons for encouraging their growth in certain places, Noel. But to give them back their prophet—it doesn't make sense."

Vorst tapped a stud in his desk. A compartment opened and he drew forth the Book of Lazarus, the heretic scripture. Kirby seemed a little startled to find it here, in the stronghold of the movement.

"You've read this, haven't you?" Vorst asked.

"Of course."

"It's enough to make you weep. How my shameless underlings hunted down this great and good man David Lazarus and did away with him. One of the most blasphemous acts since the Crucifixion, eh? The blot on our record. We're the villains in the Lazarus story. Now here's Lazarus, pickled on Mars for the last sixty years. Not physically annihilated after all, despite what this book says. Fine. Splendid! We throw all the resources of Santa Fe into the task of restoring him to life. The grand ecumenical gesture. Surely you know that it's my hope to reunite the sundered branches of our movement."

Kirby's eyes flickered brilliantly. "You've been saying that for sixty or seventy years, Noel. Ever since the Harmonists split away. But do you mean it?"

"I'm sincere in all things," said Vorst lightly. "Of course I'd take them back. On my terms, naturally—but they'd be welcome. We all serve the same ends in different ways. Did you ever know Lazarus?"

"Not really. I wasn't very important in the Brotherhood when he died."

"I forget that," Vorst said. "It's hard for me to keep everyone positioned in his temporal matrix. I keep sliding forward and backward. But certainly—you were coming to the top as Lazarus was moving away. I respected that man, Kirby. I grieved when he died, wrongheaded as he was. I intend to redeem the Brotherhood from its stain by bringing Lazarus back to life. He's appropriately named, wouldn't you say?"

Kirby picked up a bright metallic sphere from the desk, a paperweight of some sort, and fingered it. Vorst waited. He kept the sphere there so that his visitors could handle it and discharge their tensions into it; he knew that for many who came before him an interview with Vorst was like a trip to the top of Mount Sinai to hear the Law. Vorst found it charming. He watched Reynolds Kirby struggling with himself.

At length Kirby—the only man on the whole planet who could use Vorst's first name to him—said thickly, "Damn it, Noel, what kind of game are you playing?"

"Game?"

"You sit there with that grin on your lips, telling me you're going to revive Lazarus, and I can see you juggling world-lines like billiard balls, and I don't know what it's all about. What's your motive? Isn't this man better off dead?"

"No. Dead he's a symbol. Alive he can be manipulated. That's all I'll say." Vorst's blazing eyes found Kirby's troubled ones and held them. "Do you think I'm senile at last, perhaps? That I've held the plan in my mind so long that it's rotted in there? I know what I'm doing. I need Lazarus alive, or—or I wouldn't have begun this. Get in touch with Nat Weiner. Gain possession of the vault, I don't care how. We'll do our work on Lazarus here at Santa Fe."

"All right, Noel. Whatever you say."

"Trust me."

"What else can I do?"

Kirby wheeled himself out of the room. Vorst, relaxing,

fed hormones to his bloodstream and closed his eyes. The world wavered. For an instant he found himself drifting, and it was 2071 all over again, and he was building cobalt-60 reactors in a sordid basement and renting little rooms as chapels for his cult. He recoiled, and was whirled forward, dizzyingly, toward the border of now and a little beyond it. Vorst was a low-grade esper, his skills humble indeed, but occasionally his mind did strange things. He looked toward the brink of tomorrow and desperately anchored himself.

With a decisive jab of his fingers Vorst opened his desk-communicator and spoke briefly to an intern in the burnout ward, without identifying himself. Yes, the Founder was told, there was an esper on the verge of burnout. No, she wasn't likely to survive.

"Get her ready," Vorst said. "The Founder's going to visit her."

Vorst's assistants clustered around, readying him for his journey. The old man refused to accept immobility and insisted on leading the most active kind of existence possible. A dropshaft took him to ground level, and then, sheltered by the cavalcade of flunkies that accompanied him everywhere, the Founder crossed the main plaza of the compound and entered the burnout ward.

Half a dozen sick espers, segregated by thick walls and shielded by protective members of their own kind, lay at the verge of death. There were always those for whom the powers proved overwhelming, those who eventually seized more voltage than they could handle and were destroyed. From the very beginning Vorst had concentrated on saving them, for these were the espers he needed most badly. The salvage record was good nowadays. But not good enough.

Vorst knew why the burnouts happened. The ones who went were the floaters, insecurely anchored in their own time. They drifted back, forth, seesawing from past to present, unable to control their movements, building up a charge of temporal force that ultimately blasted their minds. It was a dizziness of the time-sense, a deadly vertigo. Vorst himself had felt flashes of it. For ten years, nearly a century ago, he had considered himself insane, until he understood. He had seen the edges of time, a vision of futurity that had shattered him and remade him, and that, he knew, had been only a hint of what the real espers experienced.

The burnout case was young and female and Oriental: a fatal combination, it seemed. A good eighty percent of the burnouts were of Mongoloid stock, generally adolescent girls. Those who had the trait didn't last far into adulthood. This one must have been about sixteen, though it was hard to tell; she could have been anywhere from twelve to twenty-five. She lay twisting on the bed, her body almost bare, clawing at the bedclothes in her agony. Sweat gleamed on her yellow-brown skin. She arched her back, grimaced, fell back. Her breasts, revealed by the disarray of her robe, were like a child's.

Blue-clad Vorsters, awed by the presence of the Founder, flanked the bed. Vorst said, "She'll be gone in an hour, won't she?"

Someone nodded. Vorst moved himself closer to the bed. He seized the girl's arm in his wizened fingers. Another esper stepped in, placed one hand on Vorst, the other on the girl, providing the link that Vorst required. Suddenly he was in contact with the dying girl.

Her brain was on fire. She jolted backward and forward in time, and Vorst jolted with her, drawn along as a hitchhiker. Light flared in his mind, as though lightning danced about him. Yesterday and tomorrow became one. His thin body quivered like a buffeted reed. Images danced like demons, shadowy figures out of the past, dark avatars of tomorrow. *Tell me, tell me, tell me,* Vorst implored. *Show me the path!* He stood at the threshold of knowledge. For seventy years he had moved step by step this way, using the contorted and tortured bodies of these burnouts as his bridges to tomorrow, pulling himself forward by his own bootstraps along the world-line of his great plan.

Let me see, Vorst begged.

The figure of David Lazarus bestrode the pattern of tomorrow, as Vorst knew it would. Lazarus stood like a colossus, come forth to an unexpected resurrection, holding his arms out to the green-robed brethren of his heresy. Vorst shivered. The image wavered and was gone. The frail hand of the Founder relaxed its grip.

"She's dead," Vorst said. "Take me away."

four

One old man had given the word, and another obeyed, and a third was approached for a favor. Nat Weiner of the Martian Presidium was always willing to oblige his old friend Reynolds Kirby. They had known one another for more years then they cared to admit.

Weiner, like nearly all Martians, was neither Vorster nor Harmonist. Martians had little use for the cults, and steered a neutral and profitable course. On Earth, by now, the Vorsters amounted to a planetary government, since their influence was felt everywhere; it was simple good sense for Mars to retain open lines to the Vorster high command, since Mars had business to do with Earth. Venus, the planet of adapted men, was a different case. No one could be too sure what went on there, except that the Harmonist heresy had established itself pretty securely in the last thirty or forty years, and might one day speak for Venus as the Vorsters spoke for Earth. Weiner had served a tour of duty as Martian Ambassador to Venus, and he thought he understood the blueskins fairly well. He didn't like them very much. But he was past feeling any strong emotion. He had left that behind with his hundredth birthday.

At staggering cost, Reynolds Kirby in Santa Fe spoke face-to-face with Weiner, and begged a favor of him. It was twelve years since they had last met—not since Weiner's last visit to the rejuvenation centers at Santa Fe. It wasn't customary for unbelievers to be granted the use of the rejuvenation facilities there, but Kirby had arranged for Weiner and a select few of his Martian friends to come down for periodic treatments, as a favor.

Weiner understood quite clearly that Kirby was silently accepting promissory notes for those favors, and that the notes would be taken down for repayment one of these days. That was all right; the important thing was to survive. Weiner might even have been willing to become a Vorster, if he had to, in order to have access to Santa Fe. But of course that would have hurt him politically on Mars, where both Vorsters and Harmonists were generally looked upon as subversives. This way he had the benefits, without the risks, and he owed it to his old friend Kirby. Weiner would go quite a distance to repay Kirby for that service.

The Vorster said, "Have you seen the alleged Lazarus vault yet, Nat?"

"I was out there two days ago. We've got a tight security guard on it. It was my nephew who found it, you know. I'd like to kill him."

"Why?"

"All we need is finding the Harmonist muck-a-muck out by Beltran Lakes. Why couldn't you people have buried him on Venus, where his own people are?"

"What makes you think we buried him, Nat?"

"Aren't you the ones who killed him? Or put him into a freeze, or whatever you did to him?"

"It all happened before my time," Kirby said. "Only Vorst knows the real story, and maybe not even he. But surely it's Lazarus's own supporters who tucked him away in that vault, don't you think?"

"Not at all," Weiner replied. "Why would they get their own story garbled? He's their prophet. If they put him there, they should have remembered it and preached his ressurrection, yes? But they were the most surprised ones of all when he turned up." Weiner frowned. "On the other hand, the message that was recorded with him is full of Harmonist slogans. And there are Harmonist symbols on the vault. I wish I understood. Better still: I wish we'd never found him. But why are you calling, Ron?"

"Vorst wants him."

"Wants Lazarus?"

"That's right. To bring him back to life. We'll take the whole vault to Santa Fe and open it and revive him. Vorst wants to make the announcement tomorrow, all-channel hookup."

"You can't, Ron. If anybody gets him, it ought to be the Harmonists. He's their prophet. How can I hand him to you boys? You're the ones who supposedly killed him in the first place, and now—"

"And now we're going to revive him, which, as everyone knows, is beyond the capabilities of the Harmonists. They're welcome to try, if they want, but they simply don't have our kind of laboratory facilities. We're ready to revive him. Then we'll turn him over to the Harmonists and he can preach all he wants. Just let us have access to that vault."

"You're asking for a lot," Weiner said.

"We've given you a lot, Nat."

Weiner nodded. The promissory notes had fallen due, he realized.

He said, "The Harmonists will have my head for this."

"Your head's pretty tightly attached, Nat. Find a way to give us the vault. Vorst will be pretty rough on us all if you don't."

Weiner sighed. "His will be done."

But how, the Martian wondered when contact had broken? By *force majeure?* Hand over the vault and to hell with public opinion? And if Venus got nasty about it? There hadn't been an interplanetary war yet, but perhaps the time was ripe. Certainly the Harmonists wanted—and had every right to have—their own founder's body. Just last week that convert Martell, the one who had come to Venus to plant a Vorster cell and ended up in the Harmonist camp, had been here to see the vault, Weiner thought, and had tentatively sketched out a plan for taking possession. Martell and his boss Mondschein would explode when they found out that the relic of Lazarus was being shipped to Santa Fe.

It would have to be handled delicately.

Weiner's mind whirred and clicked like a computer, presenting and rejecting alternate possibilities, opening and closing one circuit after another. It was not seniority alone that kept the Martian in power. He was agile. He had gained considerably in craftiness since the night when, a drunken young yokel, he ran amok in New York City.

Three hours and a great many thousand dollars' worth of interplanetary calls later, Weiner had his solution worked out satisfactorily.

The vault was Martian governmental property, as an artifact. Therefore Mars had an important voice in its disposal. However, the Martian government recognized the unique symbolic value of this discovery, and thus proposed to consult with religious authorities of the other worlds. A committee would be formed: three Harmonists, three Vorsters, and three Martians of Weiner's selection. Presumably the Harmonists and Vorsters would look out only for their own cult's welfare, and the Martians on the committee would maintain an imperturbable neutrality, assuring an impartial judgment.

Of course.

The committee would meet to deliberate on the fate of the vault. The Harmonists, naturally, would claim it for themselves. The Vorsters, having made public their offer to employ all their superscience to bring Lazarus back to life, would ask to be given a chance to do so. The Martians would weigh all the possibilities.

Then, Weiner thought, would come the vote.

One of the Martians would vote with the Harmonists—for appearance's sake. The other two would come out in favor of letting the Vorsters work on the sleeper, under rigorous supervision to prevent any hanky-panky. The five-to-four vote would give the vault to Vorst. Mondschein would yelp, of course. But the terms of the agreement would allow a couple of Harmonist representatives to get inside the secret labs at Santa Fe for a little while, and that would soothe them somewhat. There would be a little grumbling, but if Kirby kept his word, Lazarus would be revived and turned over to his partisans, and how could the Harmonists possibly object to that?

Weiner smiled. There was no problem so knotty that it couldn't be untied. Given a little thought, that is. He felt pleased with himself. If he had been forty years younger, he might have gone out for a roistering celebration. But not now.

five

"Don't go," Martell said.

"Suspicious?" Christopher Mondschein asked. "It's a chance to see their setup. I haven't been in Santa Fe since I was a boy. Why shouldn't I go?"

"There's no telling what might happen to you there. They'd love to get their hands on you. You're the kingpin of the whole Venusian movement."

"And they'll lase me to ashes with three planets watching, eh? Be realistic, Nicholas. When the Pope visits Mecca, they take good care of him. I'm in no danger in Santa Fe."

"What about the espers? They'll scan you."

"I'll have Neerol with me as a mindshield," Mondschein said. "They won't get a thing. I'll stack him up against any esper they have. Besides, I have nothing to hide from Noel Vorst. You of all people ought to realize that. We took you in, even though you were loaded with Vorster spy-commands. It was in our interest to tell Vorst how far we had gone."

Martell took a different approach. "By going to Santa Fe you're putting the blessing of our order on this alleged Lazarus."

"Now you sound like Brother Emory! Are you telling me it's a phony?"

"I'm telling you that we ought to treat it as one. It contradicts our own legend of Lazarus. It may be a Vorster plant calculated to throw us into confusion. What do we do when they hand us a walking, talking Lazarus and let us try to reshape our entire order around him?"

"It's a touchy matter, Nicholas. We've built our faith on the existence of a holy martyr. Now, if he's suddenly unmartyred—"

"Exactly. It'll crush us."

"I doubt that," Mondschein said. The old Harmonist touched his gills lightly, nervously. "You aren't looking far enough ahead, Nicholas. The Vorsters have outmaneuvered us so far, I admit. They've gained possession of this Lazarus, and they're about to give him back to us. Very embarrassing, but what can we do? However, the next moves are ours. If he dies, we simply revise our writings a bit. If he lives and tries to meddle, we reveal that he's some sort of simulacrum cooked up by the Vorsters to do mischief, and destroy him. Score a point for us—our original story stands and we reveal the Vorsters as sinister schemers."

"And if he's really Lazarus?" Martell asked.

Mondschein glowered. "Then we have a prophet on our hands, Brother Nicholas. It's a risk we take. I'm going to Santa Fe."

six

_____

On Earth, the Noel Vorst Center throbbed with more-than-usual activity as preparations continued for the arrival of the cargo from Mars. An entire block of the laboratory grounds had been set aside for the resuscitation of Lazarus. For the first time since the founding of the Center video cameras would be allowed to show the worlds a little of its inner workings. The place would be full of strangers—even a delegation of Harmonists. To old-line Vorsters like Reynolds Kirby, that was almost unthinkable. Furtiveness had become a matter of course for him. The command, though, had come from Vorst himself, and no one could quarrel with the Founder. "I believe that it's time to lift the lid a little," Vorst had said.

Kirby was doing some lid-lifting of his own as the great day drew near. He was troubled by certain blanks in his own memory, and by virtue of his rank as second-in-command he went searching through the Vorster archives to fill them in. The trouble was, Kirby could not remember much about David Lazarus's pre-martyrdom career, and he felt that it was important to know something more than the official story. Who was Lazarus, anyway? How had he entered the Vorster picture—and how had he left it?

Kirby himself had enrolled in 2077, kneeling before the Blue Fire of a cobalt reactor in New York. As a new convert, he had not been concerned with the politics of the hierarchy, but simply with the values the cult had to offer:

stability, the hope of long life, the dream of reaching the stars by harnessing the abilities of espers. Kirby was willing to see mankind explore the other solar systems, but he did not make that accomplishment the central yearning of his life. Nor did the chance of immortality—the chief bait for millions of Vorster converts—seem all that delicious to him.

What drew him to the movement, at the age of forty, was merely the discipline that it offered. His pleasant life lacked structure, and the world about him was such chaos that he fled from it into one synthetic paradise after another. Along came Vorst offering a sleek new belief that snared Kirby totally. For the first few months he was content to be a worshiper. Soon he was an acolyte. And then, his natural organizational abilities demonstrating themselves, he found himself moving rapidly upward in the movement from post to post until by the time he was eighty he was Vorst's right hand, and very much concerned with his own personal survival.

According to the official story, the martyrdom of David Lazarus had taken place in 2090. Kirby had been a Vorster for thirteen years then, and was a District Supervisor in charge of thousands of Brothers.

So far as he could remember, he had never even heard of Lazarus as of 2090.

A few years later the Harmonists, the heretical movement, had begun gaining strength, decking themselves in green robes and scoffing at the craftily secular power-orientation of the Vorsters. They claimed to be followers of the martyred Lazarus, but even then, Kirby thought, they hadn't talked much about Lazarus. Only afterward, as Harmonist power mounted and they stole Venus from Vorst, did they push the Lazarus mythos particularly hard. *Why is it,* Kirby wondered, *that I who was a contemporary of Lazarus should never have heard his name?*

He walked toward the archives building.

It was a milk-white geodesic dome, sheeted with some toothy fabric that gave it a sharkskin surface texture. Kirby passed through a tiled tunnel, identified himself to the robot guardians, moved toward and past a sphincter-door, and found himself in the olive-green room where the records were kept. He activated a query-stud and demanded knowledge.

LAZARUS, DAVID.

Drums whirled in the depths of the earth. Memory films came around, offered themselves to the kiss of the scanner, and sent images floating upward to the waiting Kirby. Glowing yellow print appeared on the reader-screen.

A potted biography, scanty and inadequate:

BORN 13 March 2051

EDUCATION Primary Secondary Chicago, A.B. Harvard '72, Ph.D. (Anthropology) Harvard '75.

PHYSICAL DESCRIPTION (1/1/88) 6 ft. 3 ins., 179 pounds, dark eyes and hair, no dis. scars.

AFFILIATION Joined Cambridge chapel 4/11/71. Acolyte status conferred 7/17/73. . . .

There followed a list of the successive stages by which Lazarus had risen through the hierarchy, culminating with the simple entry, DEATH 2/9/90.

That was all. It was a lean, spare record, not a word of elaboration, no appended commendations such as Kirby knew festooned his own record, no documentation of Lazarus's disagreement with Vorst. Nothing. It was the sort of record, Kirby thought uncomfortably, that anyone could have tapped out in five minutes and inserted in the archives . . . yesterday.

He prodded the memory banks, hoping to fish up some added detail about the arch-heretic. He found nothing. It was not really valid cause for suspicion; Lazarus had been dead for a long time, and probably the record-keeping had been sketchier in those early days. But it was upsetting, all the same. Kirby made his way out of the building. Acolytes stared at him as though Vorst himself had gone striding by. No doubt some of them felt the temptation to drop to their knees before him. *If they only knew,* Kirby thought darkly, *how ignorant I am. After seventy-five years with Vorst. If they only knew.*

seven

The glass vault of David Lazarus, transported intact at considerable expense from Mars, rested in the center of the operating room, under the watchful eyes of the video cameras mounted in the walls and ceiling. A carefully planted forest of equipment surrounded the vault: polygraphs, compressors, centrifuges, surgistats, scanners, enzyme calibrators, laser scalpels, retractors, impacters, thorax rods, cerebral tacks, a heart-and-lung bypass, kidney surrogates, mortmains, biopticons, elsevirs, a Helium II pressure generator, and a monstrous, glowering cryostat. The display was impressive, and it was meant to be. Vorster science was on display here, and every awesome-looking superfluity in the place had its part in the orchestration of the effects.

Vorst himself was not present. That, too, was part of the orchestration. He and Kirby were watching the event from Vorst's office. The highest-ranking member of the Brotherhood present was plump, cheerful Capodimonte, a District Supervisor. Beside him stood Christopher Mondschein of the Harmonists. Mondschein and Capodimonte had known each other briefly during Mondschein's short, spectacularly unsuccessful career as a Santa Fe acolyte in 2095. Now, though, the Harmonist was a terrifying figure, his changed body concealed by a breathing-suit but still nightmarish and grotesque. A native-born Venusian, looking even more bizarre, clung to Mondschein like a skin graft. The visiting Harmonists seemed tense and grim.

169

The television commentator said, "It's already been determined that the atmosphere of the vault is a mixture of inert gases, mainly argon. Lazarus himself is in a nutrient bath. Espers have detected signs of life. The tumblers of the vault lock were opened yesterday in the presence of the delegation of Venusian Harmonists. Now the inerts are being piped out, and soon the sensitive instruments of the surgeons will reach the sleeping man and begin the infinitely complex process of restoring the life-impulses."

Vorst laughed.

Kirby said, "Isn't that what'll happen?"

"More or less. Exept the man's as alive as he'll ever be, right now. All they need to do is open the vault and yank him out."

"That wouldn't be very dramatic."

"Probably not," the Founder agreed. Vorst folded his hands across his belly, feeling the artificials throbbing mildly inside. The commentator reeled off acres of descriptive prose. The spidery array of instruments surrounding the vault was in motion now, arms and tendrils waving like the limbs of some being of many bodies. Vorst kept his eyes on the altered face of Christopher Mondschein. He hadn't really believed that Mondschein would return to Santa Fe. An admirable person, the old man thought. He had borne adversity well, considering how he had been bamboozled into his life's career almost sixty years ago.

"The vault's open," Kirby said.

"So I observe. Now watch the mummy of King Tut rise and walk."

"You're very lighthearted about this, Noel."

"Mmmm," the Founder said. A smile flickered on his thin lips for a moment. He made minute adjustments to his hormone flow. On the screen the vault opening was almost completely obscured by the instruments that had dived into the chamber to embrace the sleeper.

Suddenly there was faint motion in the vault. Lazarus stirred! The martyr returned!

"Time for my grand entrance," Vorst murmured.

All was arranged. A glistening tunnel transported him

swiftly to the operating room. Kirby did not follow. The Founder's chair rolled serenely into the room just as the figure of David Lazarus groped its way out of sixty years of sleep and rose to a sitting position.

A quivering hand pointed. A rusty voice strained for coherence.

"V-V-Vorst!" Lazarus gasped.

The Founder smiled benevolently, lifted his fleshless arm in greeting and blessing. Delicately, an unseen hand slipped a control rod and the Blue Fire flickered along the walls of the room to provide the proper theatrical touch. Christopher Mondschein, his altered face impassive behind his breathing-mask, clenched his fists angrily as the glow enveloped him.

Vorst said, "And there is light, before and beyond our vision, for which we give thanks.

"And there is heat, for which we are humble.

"And there is power, for which we count ourselves blessed. . . .

"Welcome to life, David Lazarus. In the strength of the spectrum, the quantum, and the holy angstrom, peace, and forgive those who did evil to you!"

Lazarus stood. His hands found and grasped the rim of his vault. Inconceivable emotions distorted his face. He muttered, "I—I've slept."

"Sixty years, David. And those who rebuked me and followed you have grown strong. See? See the green robes? Venus is yours. You head a mighty army. Go to them, David. Give them counsel. I restore you to them. You are my gift to your followers. *And he that was dead came forth . . . loose him, and let him go.*"

Lazarus did not reply. Mondschein stood agape, leaning heavily on the Venusian at his side. Kirby, watching the screen, felt a tingle of awe that washed away his skepticism for the moment. Even the chatter of the television commentator was stilled by the miracle.

The glow of the Blue Fire engulfed all, rising higher and higher, like the flames of the Twilight reaching toward Valhalla. And in the midst of it all stood Noel Vorst, the Founder, the First Immortal, serene and radiant, his ancient body erect, his eyes gleaming, his hands outstretched to the man who had been dead. All that was missing was the chorus of ten thousand, singing the Hymn of the Wavelengths while a cosmic organ throbbed a paean of joy.

eight

And Lazarus lived, and walked among his people again, holding converse with them.

And Lazarus was greatly surprised.

He had slept—for a moment, for the twinkling of an eye. Now sinister blue figures surrounded him—Venusians, hooded like demons against the poisonous air of Earth—and hailed him as their prophet. All about rose Vorst's metropolis, dazzling buildings that testified to the present might of the Brotherhood of the Immanent Radiance.

The chubby Venusian—Mondschein, was it?—pressed a book into Lazarus's hands. "The Book of Lazarus," he said. "The account of your life and work."

"And death?"

"Yes, your death."

"You'll need a new edition now," Lazarus said. He smiled, but he was alone in his mirth.

He felt strong. How had muscles failed to degenerate in his long sleep? How was it that he could rise and go among men, and make vocal cords obey him, and his body withstand the strain of life?

He was alone with his followers. In a few days they would take him back to Venus with them, where he would have to live in a self-contained environment. Vorst had offered to transform him into a Venusian, but Lazarus, stunned that such things were possible at all, was not sure that he cared to become a gilled creature. He needed time

173

to ponder all this. The world he had so unexpectedly re-entered was very different from the one he had left.

Sixty-odd years. Vorst had taken over the whole planet now, it seemed. That was the direction he had been heading in back in the Eighties, when Lazarus had begun to disagree with him. Vorst had begun with a religio-scientific movement when Lazarus had joined it. Hocus-pocus with cobalt reactors, a litany of spectrum and electron, plenty of larded-on spiritualism, but at the bottom a bluntly materialistic creed whose chief come-on was the promise of long (or eternal) life. Lazarus had gone for that. But soon, feeling his strength, Vorst had begun to slide men into parliaments, take over banks, utilities, hospitals, insurance companies.

Lazarus had opposed all that. Vorst had been accessible then, and Lazarus remembered arguing with him against this deviation into finance and power politics. And Vorst had said, "The plan calls for it."

"It's a perversion of our religious motives."

"It'll get us where we want to go."

Lazarus had disagreed. Quietly, gathering a few supporters, he had established a rival group, while still nominally retaining his loyalty to Vorst. His apprenticeship with Vorst made him an expert on founding a faith. He proclaimed the reign of eternal harmony, gave his people green robes, symbols, reformist fervor, prayers, a developing liturgy. He could not say that his movement had become particularly powerful beside the Vorst machine, but at least it was a leading heresy, attracting hundreds of new followers each month. Lazarus had been looking toward a missionary movement, knowing that his ideas had a better chance of taking root on Venus and perhaps Mars than Vorst's.

And on a day in 2090 men in blue robes came to him and took him away, blanking out his guard of espers and stealing him as easily as though he had been a lump of lead. After that he knew no more, until his awakening in Santa Fe. They told him that the year was 2152 and that Venus was in the hands of his people.

Mondschein said, "Will you let yourself be changed?"

"I'm not sure yet. I'm considering it."

"It'll be difficult for you to function on Venus unless you let them adapt you."

"Perhaps I could stay on Earth," Lazarus suggested.

"Impossible. You have no power base here. Vorst's generosity will stretch only so far. He won't let you remain here after the excitement of your return dies down."

"You're right." Lazarus sighed. "I'll let myself be changed, then. I'll come to Venus and see what you've accomplished."

"You'll be pleasantly surprised," Mondschein promised.

Lazarus had already been sufficiently surprised for one incarnation. They left him, and he studied the scriptures of his faith, fascinated by the martyr's role they had written for him. A book of Harmonist history told Lazarus his own value: where the Brotherhood's religious emotions crystallized around the remote, forbidding figure of Vorst, the Harmonists could safely revere their gentle martyr. *How awkward it must be for them that I'm back,* Lazarus thought.

Vorst did not come to him while he rested in the Brotherhood's hospital. A man named Kirby came, though, frosty-faced with age, and said he was the Hemispheric Coordinator and Vorst's closest collaborator.

"I joined the Brotherhood before your disappearance," Kirby said. "Did you ever hear of me?"

"I don't believe so."

"I was only an underling," Kirby said. "I suppose you wouldn't have had reason to hear of me. But I hoped your memory would be clear, if we ever had met. I've got all these intervening years to cope with, but you can look back across a clean slate."

"My memory's fine," Lazarus said evenly. "I've got no recollection of you."

"Nor I of you."

The resuscitated man shrugged. "I worked beside Vorst.

I had disputes with him. That much is beyond question. Eventually I split with him. I founded the Harmonists. Then I—disappeared. And here I am. Do you have trouble believing in me?"

"Perhaps I've been tampered with," Kirby said. "I wish I remembered you."

Lazarus lay back. He stared at the green, rubbery walls. The instruments monitoring his life-processes whirred and clicked. There was an acrid odor in the air: asepsis at work. Kirby looked unreal. Lazarus wondered what sort of maze of pumps and trestles held him together beneath his thick, warm blue robe.

Kirby said, "You understand that you can't remain on Earth, don't you?"

"Of course."

"Life will be uncomfortable for you on Venus unless you're changed. We'll do it for you. Your own men can supervise the operation. I've talked to Mondschein about it. Are you interested?"

"Yes," Lazarus said. "Change me."

They came the next day to turn him into a Venusian. He resented the public nature of the operation, but it was idle to pretend that his life was his own any more, anyway. It would take several weeks, they said, to effect the transformation. Once it had taken months to do it. They would equip him with gills, fit him out to breathe the poisonous muck that was the atmosphere of Venus, and turn him loose. Lazarus submitted. They carved him, and put him back together again, and readied him for shipment.

Vorst came to him, feathery-voiced and shrunken, but still a commanding figure, and said, "You must realize I had no part in your kidnapping. It was totally unauthorized—the work of zealots."

"Of course."

"I appreciate diversity of opinion. My way is not necessarily the only right way. I've felt the lack of a dialogue with Venus for many years. Once you're installed there, I trust you'll be willing to communicate with me."

Lazarus said, "I won't close my mind against you,

Vorst. You've given me life. I'll listen to what you have to say. There's no reason why we can't cooperate, so long as we respect each other's sphere of interests."

"Exactly! Our goal is the same, after all. We can join forces."

"Warily," Lazarus said.

"Warily, yes. But wholeheartedly." Vorst smiled and departed.

The surgeons completed their work. Lazarus, now alien to Earth, journeyed to Venus with Mondschein and the rest of the Harmonist retinue. It was in the nature of a triumphant homecoming, if one can be said to come home to a place where one has never been before.

Green-robed brethren with bluish-purple skins greeted him. Lazarus saw the Harmonist shrines, the holy ikons of his order. They had carried the spiritualistic element further than he had ever visualized, practically deifying him, but Lazarus did not intend to correct that. He knew how precarious his position was. There were men of entrenched power in his organization who secretly might not welcome a prophet's return, and who might give him a second martyrdom if he challenged their vested interests. Lazarus moved warily.

"We have made great progress with the espers," Mondschein told him. "We're considerably ahead of Vorst's work in that line, so far as we know."

"Do you have telekinesis yet?"

"For twenty years. We're building the power steadily. Another generation—"

"I'd like a demonstration."

"We have one planned," Mondschein said.

They showed him what they could do. To reach into a block of wood and set its molecules dancing in flame—to move a boulder through the sky—to whisk themselves from place to place—yes, it was impressive, it defied comprehension. It certainly must be beyond the abilities of the Brotherhood on Earth.

The Venusian espers cavorted for Lazarus, hour after hour. Mondschein, sedate and complacent, gleamed with satisfaction, spoke of thresholds, levitation, telekinetic impetus, fulcrums of unity, and other matters that left Lazarus baffled but encouraged.

He who had returned pointed to the gray band of clouds that hid the heavens.

"How soon?" Lazarus asked.

"We're not ready for interstellar transport yet," Mondschein replied. "Not even interplanetary, though in theory one shouldn't be any harder than the other. We're working on it. Give us time. We'll succeed."

"Can we do it without Vorst's help?" Lazarus asked.

Mondschein's complacence was punctured. "What kind of help can *he* give us? I've told you, we're a generation ahead of his espers."

"And will espers be enough? Perhaps he can supply what we're missing. A joint venture—Harmonists and Vorsters collaborating—don't you think the possibilities are worth exploring, Brother Christopher?"

Mondschein smiled blandly. "Why, yes, yes, of course. Certainly they're worth exploring. It's an approach we hadn't considered, I admit, but you give us a fresh insight into our problems. I'd like to discuss the matter with you further, after you've had a chance to settle down here."

Lazarus accepted Mondschein's flow of words graciously. He had not, though, been away so long that he had forgotten how to read the meanings behind the meanings.

He knew when he was being humored.

nine

At Santa Fe, with the unaccustomed invasion of Harmonists at its end, things returned to normal. Lazarus was come forth and loose upon the worlds, and the television men had retreated, and work went on. The tests, the experiments, the probing of the mysteries of life and mind—the ceaseless tasks of the Vorster inner movement.

Kirby said, "Was there ever really a David Lazarus, Noel?"

Vorst glowered up at him out of a thermoplastic cocoon. Hardly had the surgeons finished with Lazarus than they had gone to work on the Founder, who was suffering from an aneurysm in a twice-reconstituted blood vessel. Sensors had nailed the spot, subcutaneous scoops had exposed it, microtapes had been slammed into place, a network of thread and looping polymers replacing the dangerous bubble. Vorst was no stranger to such surgery.

He said, "You saw Lazarus with your own eyes, Kirby."

"I saw something come out of that vault and stand up and talk rationally. I had conversations with it. I watched it get turned into a Venusian. That doesn't mean it was real. You could build a Lazarus, couldn't you, Noel?"

"If I wanted to. But why would I want to?"

"That's obvious. To get control of the Harmonists."

"If I had designs against the Harmonists," Vorst explained patiently, "I would have blotted them out fifty

179

years ago, before they took Venus. They're all right. That young man, Mondschein—he's developed nicely."

"He isn't young, Noel. He's at least eighty."

"A child."

"Will you tell me whether Lazarus is genuine?"

Vorst's eyes fluttered in irritation. "He's genuine, Kirby. Satisfied?"

"Who put him in that vault?"

"His own followers, I suppose."

"Who then forgot all about it?"

"Well, perhaps my men did it. Without authorization. Without telling me. It happened a long time ago." Vorst's hands moved in quick, agitated gestures. "How can I remember everything? He was found. We brought him back to life. I gave him to them. You're annoying me, Kirby."

Kirby realized that he was treading a field salted with mines. He had pushed Vorst as far as Vorst could be pushed, and anything further would be disastrous. Kirby had seen other men presume too deeply on their closeness to Vorst, and he had seen that closeness imperceptibly withdrawn.

"I'm sorry," Kirby said.

Vorst's displeasure vanished. "You overrate my deviousness, Kirby. Stop worrying about Lazarus's past. Simply consider the future. I've given him to the Harmonists. He'll be valuable to them, whether they think so now or not. They're indebted to me. I've planted a good, heavy obligation on them. Don't you think that's useful? They owe me something now. When the right time comes, I'll cash that in."

Kirby remained mute. He sensed that somehow Vorst had altered the balance of power between the two cults, that the Harmonists, who had been on a rising curve ever since gaining possession of Venus and its rich lode of espers, had been brought to heel. But he did not know how it had been accomplished, and he did not care to try again to learn.

Vorst was using his communicator. He looked up at Kirby.

"They've got another burnout," he said. "I want to be there. Come with me, yes?"

"Of course," Kirby said.

He accompanied the Founder through the maze of tubes. They emerged in the burnout ward. An esper lay dying, a boy this time, perhaps Hawaiian, his body jerking as though he were skewered on cords.

Vorst said, "A pity you've got no esping, Kirby. You'd see a glimpse of tomorrow."

"I'm too old to regret it now," Kirby said.

Vorst rolled forward and gestured to a waiting esper. The link was made. Kirby watched. What was Vorst experiencing now? The Founder's lips were moving, almost writhing in a kind of sneer, pulling back from the gums with each twitch of the esper's body. The boy was shuttling along the time-track, so they said. To Kirby that meant nothing. And Vorst, somehow, was shuttling with him, seeing a clouded view of the world on the other side of the wall of time.

Now—now—back—forth—

For a moment it seemed to Kirby that he, too, had joined the linkup and was riding the time-track as the esper's other passenger. Was that the chaos of yesterday? And the golden glow of tomorrow? Now—now—*damn you, you old schemer, what have you done to me?*— Lazarus, rising above all else, Lazarus who wasn't even real, only some android stew cooked up in an underground laboratory at Vorst's command, a useful puppet, Kirby thought, Lazarus had grasped tomorrow and was stealing it—

The contact broke. The esper was dead.

"We've wasted another one," Vorst muttered. The Founder looked at Kirby. "Are you sick?" he asked.

"No. Tired."

"Get some rest. Six history spools and climb into a relaxer tank. We can ease up now. Lazarus is off our hands."

Kirby nodded. Someone drew a sheet over the dead esper's body. In an hour the boy's neurons would be in refrigeration somewhere in an adjoining building. Slowly, walking as if eight centuries and not just one weighed upon him, Kirby followed Vorst from the room. Night had fallen, and the stars over New Mexico had their peculiar hard brightness, and Venus, low against the mountainous horizon, was the brightest of all. They had their Lazarus, up there. They had lost a martyr and had gained a prophet. And, Kirby was beginning to realize, the whole tribe of heretics had been swept neatly into Vorst's pocket. The old man was damnable. Kirby huddled down into his robe and kept pace, with an effort, as Vorst wheeled himself toward his office. His head ached from that brief, unfathomable contact with the esper. But in ten minutes it was better.

He thought of going to a chapel to pray. But what was the use? Why kneel before the Blue Fire? He need only go to Vorst for a blessing—Vorst, his mentor for almost eight decades, Vorst, who could make him feel still like a child, Vorst, who had brought Lazarus forth from the dead.

FIVE

To Open the Sky
2164

─────────────────

one

~~~~~~

The surgical amphitheater was a chilly horseshoe lit by a pale violet glow. At the north end, windows on the level of the second gallery admitted frosty New Mexico sunlight. From where he sat, overlooking the operating table, Noel Vorst could see the bluish mountains in the middle distance beyond the confines of the research center. The mountains did not interest him. Neither did what was taking place on the operating table. But he kept his lack of interest to himself.

Vorst had not needed to attend the operation in person, of course. He knew already that a successful outcome was improbable, and so did everyone else. But the Founder was 144 years old, and thought it useful to appear in public as often as his strength could sustain the effort. It did not do to have people think he had lapsed into senility.

Down below, the surgeons were clustered about a bare brain. Vorst had watched them lift the dome of a skull and thrust their scalpels of light deep into the wrinkled gray mass. There were ten billion neurons in that block of tissue, and an infinity of axonal terminals and dendritic receptors. The surgeons hoped to rearrange the synaptic nets of that brain, altering the protein-molecular switchgear to render the patient more useful to Vorst's plan.

Folly, the old man thought. He hid his pessimism and sat quietly, listening to the pulsing of the blood in his own glossy artificial arteries.

What they were doing down there was remarkable, of course. Summoning all the resources of modern microsurgery, the leading men of the Noel Vorst Center for the Biological Sciences were altering the protein-protein molecular recognition patterns within a human brain. Twist the circuits about a bit; change the transsynaptic structures to build a better link between pre- and postsynaptic membranes; shunt individual synaptic inputs from one dendritic tree to another; in short, reprogram the brain to make it capable of doing what Noel Vorst wanted it to be capable of doing.

Which was to serve as the propulsive force needed to hurl a team of explorers across the gulf of light-years to another star.

It was an extraordinary project. For some fifty years the surgeons here at Vorst's Santa Fe research center had prepared for it by meddling with the brains of cats and monkeys and dolphins. Now they had at last begun operating on human subjects. The patient on the table was a middle-grade esper, a precog with poor timebinding ability; his life expectancy was on the order of six months, and then a burnout could be anticipated. The precog knew all about that, which was why he had volunteered to be the subject. The most skilful surgeons in the world were at work on him.

There were only two things wrong with the project, Vorst knew:

It was not likely to succeed.

And it was not at all necessary in the first place.

You did not tell a group of dedicated men, however, that their life's work was pointless. Besides, there was always the faint hope that they might artificially create a pusher—a telekinetic—down there. So Vorst dutifully attended the operation. The men on the amphitheater floor knew that the Founder's numinous presence was with them. Though they did not look up toward the gallery where Vorst sat, they knew the withered but still vigorous old man was smiling benignly down on them, cushioned against the pull of Earth by the webfoam cradle that sheltered his ancient limbs.

The lenses of his eyes were synthetic. The coils of his intestines had been fashioned from laboratory polymers. The stoutly pumping heart came from an organ bank. Little remained of the original Noel Vorst but the brain itself, which was intact though awash with the anticoagulants that preserved it from disabling strokes.

"Are you comfortable, sir?" the pale young acolyte at his side asked.

"Perfectly. Are you?"

The acolyte smiled at Vorst's little joke. He was only twenty years old, and full of pride because it was his turn to accompany the Founder on his daily round. Vorst liked young people about him. They were tremendously in awe of him, naturally, but they managed to be warm and respectful without canonizing him. Within his body there throbbed the contributions of many a young Vorster volunteer: a film of lung tissue from one, a retina from another, kidneys from a pair of twins. He was a patchwork man, who carried the flesh of his movement about with him.

The surgeons were bending low over the exposed brain down there. Vorst could not see what they were doing. A pickup embedded in a surgical instrument relayed the scene to a lambent screen on the level of the viewing gallery, but even the enlarged image did not tell Vorst much. Baffled and bored, he retained his look of lively interest all the same.

Quietly he pushed a communicator stud on his armrest and said, "Is Coordinator Kirby going to get here soon?"

"He's talking to Venus, sir."

"Who's he speaking to? Lazarus or Mondschein?"

"Mondschein, sir. I'll tell him to come to you as soon as he's off."

Vorst smiled. Protocol suggested that such high-level negotiations be carried on at the administrative level, between the executives and not between the prophets. So the second-in-commands were speaking: Hemispheric Coordinator Reynolds Kirby on behalf of the Vorsters of Earth, and Christopher Mondschein for the Harmonists who ran

Venus. But in time it would be necessary to close the deal with a conference between those most closely in tune with the Eternal Oneness, and that would be the task of Vorst and Lazarus.

. . . to close the deal . . .

A tremor pulled Vorst's right hand into a sudden claw. The acolyte swung around attentively, ready to jab buttons until he had restored the Founder's metabolic equilibrium. Grimly Vorst compelled the hand to relax.

"I'm all right," he insisted.

. . . to open the sky . . .

They were so close to the end now that it had all begun to seem like a dream. A century of scheming, playing chess with unborn antagonists, rearing a fantastic edifice of theocracy on a single slender, arrogant hope—

Was it madness, Vorst wondered, to wish to reshape the pattern of history?

Was it monstrous, he asked himself, to succeed?

On the operating table, the patient's leg came swimming up out of a sea of swathing and kicked fitfully and convulsively at the air. The anesthetist's fingers played over his console, and the esper who was standing by for such an emergency went into silent action. There was a flurry of activity about the table.

In that moment a tall, weathered-looking old man entered the gallery and presented himself to Vorst.

"How's the operation going?" Reynolds Kirby asked.

"The patient just died," said Vorst. "Things seemed to be going so well, too."

two

Kirby had not expected much from the operation. He had discussed it fully with Vorst the day before; though he was no scientist himself, the Coordinator tried to keep abreast of the work being done at the research center. His own sphere of responsibility was administrative; it was Kirby's job to oversee the far-flung secular activities of the religious cult that virtually ruled the planet. It was almost ninety years since Kirby himself had been converted, and he had watched the cult grow mighty.

Political power, though it was useful to wield, was not supposed to be the Brotherhood's goal. The essence of the movement was its scientific program, centering on the facilities at Santa Fe. Here, over the decades, an unsurpassable factory of miracles had been constructed, lubricated by the cash contributions of billions of tithing Vorsters on every continent. And the miracles had been forthcoming. The regeneration processes now insured a predictable life span of three or four centuries for the newborn, perhaps more, for no one could be certain that immortality had been achieved until a few millennia of testing had elapsed. The Brotherhood could offer a reasonable facsimile of life eternal, at any rate, and that was a sufficient redemption of the promissory note on which the whole movement had been founded a hundred years before.

The other goal, though—the stars—had given the Brotherhood a harder pursuit.

Man was locked into his solar system by the limiting velocity of light. Chemical-fueled rockets and even ion-drive ships simply took too long to get about. Mars and Venus were within easy reach, but the cheerless outer planets were not, and the round trip to the nearest star would take a few decades by current technology, nine years even at the very best. So man had transformed Mars into a habitable world, and he had transformed himself into something capable of inhabiting Venus. He mined the moons of Jupiter and Saturn, paid occasional visits to Pluto, and sent robots down to examine Mercury and the gas giants. And looked hopelessly to the stars.

The laws of relativity governed the motions of real bodies through real space, but they did not necessarily apply to the events of the paranormal world. To Noel Vorst, it had seemed that the only route to the stars was the extrasensory one. So he had gathered espers of all varieties at Santa Fe, and for generations now had carried on breeding programs and genetic manipulations. The Brotherhood had spawned an interesting variety of espers, but none with the talent of transporting physical bodies through space. While on Venus the telekinetic mutation had happened spontaneously, an ironic byproduct of the adaptation of human life to that world.

Venus was beyond direct Vorster control. The Harmonists of Venus had the pushers that Vorst needed to reach into the galaxy. They showed little interest, though, in collaborating with the Vorsters on an expedition. For weeks now Reynolds Kirby had been negotiating with his opposite number on Venus, attempting to bring about an agreement.

Meanwhile the surgeons at Santa Fe had never given up their dream of creating pushers out of Earthmen, thus making the cooperation of the unpredictable Venusians unnecessary. The synaptic-rearrangement project, flowering at last, had come to the stage where a human subject would go under the beam.

"It won't work," Vorst had said to Kirby. "They're still fifty years away from anything."

"I don't understand it, Noel. The Venusians have the gene for telekinesis, don't they? Why can't we just duplicate it? Considering all we've done with the nucleic acids—"

Vorst smiled. "There's no 'gene for telekinesis,' as such, you know. It's part of a constellation of genetic patterns. We've been trying consciously to duplicate it for thirty years, and we aren't even close. We've also been trying a random approach, since that's how the Venusians got the ability. No luck there, either. And then there's this synapse business: alter the brain itself, not the genes. That may get us somewhere, eventually. But I can't wait another fifty years."

"You'll live that long, certainly."

"Yes," Vorst agreed, "but I still can't wait any longer. The Venusians have the men we need. It's time to win them to our purposes."

Patiently Kirby had wooed the heretics. There were signs of progress in the negotiations now. In view of the failure of the operation, the need for an agreement with Venus was more urgent.

"Come with me," Vorst said, as the dead patient was wheeled away. "They're testing that gargoyle today, and I want to watch."

Kirby followed the Founder out of the amphitheater. Acolytes were close by in case of trouble. Vorst, these days, rarely tried to walk any more, and rolled along in his cradling net of webfoam. Kirby still preferred to use his feet, though he was nearly as ancient as Vorst. The sight of the two of them promenading through the plazas of the research center always stirred attention.

"You aren't disturbed over the failure just now?" Kirby asked.

"Why should I be? I told you it was too soon for success."

"What about this gargoyle? Any hope?"

"Our hope," Vorst said quietly, "is Venus. They already have the pushers."

"Then why keep trying to develop them here?"

"Momentum. The Brotherhood hasn't slowed down in a hundred years. I'm not closing any avenues now. Not even the hopeless ones. It's all a matter of momentum."

Kirby shrugged. For all the power he held in the organization—and his powers were immense—he had never felt that he held any real initiative. The plans of the movement were generated, as they had been from the first, by Noel Vorst. He and only he knew what game he was playing. And if Vorst died this afternoon, with the game unfinished? What would happen to the movement then? Run on its own momentum? To what end, Kirby wondered.

They entered a squat, glittering little building of irradiated green foamglass. An awed hush preceded them: Vorst was coming! Men in blue robes came out to greet the Founder. They led him to the room in the rear where the gargoyle was kept. Kirby kept pace, ignoring the acolytes who were ready to catch him if he stumbled.

The gargoyle was sitting enmeshed in lacy restraining ribbons. He was not a pretty sight. Thirteen years old, three feet tall, grotesquely deformed, deaf, crippled, his corneas clouded, his skin pebbled and granulated. A mutant, though not one produced by any laboratory; this was Hurler's Syndrome, a natural and congenital error of metabolism, first identified scientifically two and a half centuries before. The unlucky parents had brought the hapless monster to a chapel of the Brotherhood in Stockholm, hoping that by bathing him in the Blue Fire of the cobalt reactor his defects would be cured. The defects had not been cured, but an esper at the chapel had detected latent talents in the gargoyle, and so he was here to be probed and tested. Kirby felt a shiver of revulsion.

"What causes such a thing?" he asked the medic at his elbow.

"Abnormal genes. They produce metabolic error that results in an accumulation of mucopolysaccharides in the tissues of the body."

Kirby nodded solemnly. "And is there supposed to be a direct link with esping?"

"Only coincidental," said the medic.

Vorst had moved up to study the creature at close range. The Founder's eye-shutters clicked as he peered forward. The gargoyle was humped and folded, virtually unable to move its limbs. The milky eyes held a look of pure misery. To the euthanasia heap with this one, Kirby thought. Yet Vorst hoped that such a monster would take him to the stars!

"Begin the examination," Vorst murmured.

A pair of espers came forward, general-purpose types: a slick young woman with frizzy hair, and a plump, sad-faced man. Kirby, whose own esping facilities were deficient to the point of nonexistence, watched in silence as the wordless examination commenced. What were they doing? What shafts were they aiming at the huddled creature before them? Kirby did not know, and he took comfort in the fact that Vorst probably did not know himself. The Founder wasn't much of an esper, either.

Ten minutes passed. Then the girl looked up and said, "Low-order pyrotic, mainly."

"He can push molecules about?" Vorst said. "Then he's got a shred of telekinesis."

"Only a shred," the second esper said. "Nothing that others don't have. Also low-order communication abilities. He sits there telling us to kill him."

"I'd recommend dissection," said the girl. "The subject wouldn't mind."

Kirby shuddered. These two bland espers had peered within the mind of that crippled thing, and that in itself should have been enough to shrivel their souls. To see, for an empathic moment, what it was like to be a thirteen-year-old human gargoyle, to look out upon the world through those clouded eyes—! But they were all business, these two. They had merged minds with monstrosities before.

Vorst waved his hand. "Keep him for further study. Maybe he can be guided toward usefulness. If he's really a pyrotic, take the usual precautions."

The Founder whirled his chair around and started to leave the ward. At that same moment an acolyte came hurrying in, bearing a message. He froze at the unexpected sight of Vorst wheeling toward a collision with him. Vorst smiled paternally and guided himself around the boy, who went limp with relief.

The acolyte said, "Message for you, Coordinator Kirby."

Kirby took it and jammed his thumb against the seal. The envelope popped open.

The message was from Mondschein.

"LAZARUS IS READY TO TALK TO VORST," it said.

three

———————————

Vorst said, "I was insane, you know. For something like ten years. Later I discovered what the trouble was. I was suffering from time-float."

The pallid esper girl's eyes were very round as she gazed at him. They were alone in the Founder's personal quarters. She was thin, loose-limbed, thirty years old. Strands of black hair dangled like painted straw down the sides of her face. Her name was Delphine, and in all the months that she had served Vorst's needs she had never become accustomed to his frankness. She had little chance to; when she left his office after each session, other espers erased her recollections of the visit.

She said, "Shall I turn myself on?"

"Not yet, Delphine. Do you ever think of yourself as insane? In the difficult moments, the moments when you start ranging along the time-line and don't think you'll ever get back to now?"

"It's pretty scary sometimes."

"But you get back. That's the miraculous thing. You know how many floaters I've seen burn out?" Vorst asked. "Hundreds. I'd have burned out myself, except that I'm a lousy precog. Back then, though, I kept breaking loose, drifting along the time-line. I saw the whole Brotherhood spread out before me. Call it a vision, call it a dream. I saw it, Delphine. Blurred around the edges."

"Just as you told it in your book?"

"More or less," said the Founder. "The years between 2055 and 2063—those were the years I had the visions

195

worst. When I was thirty-five, it started. I was just an ordinary technician, a nobody, and then I got what could be called divine inspiration, except all it was was a peek at my own future. I thought I was going crazy. Later I understood."

The esper was silent. Vorst shuttered his eyes. The memories glowed in him: after years of internal chaos and collapse he had come from the crucible of madness purified, aware of his purpose. He saw how he could reshape the world. More than that, he saw how he *had* reshaped the world. After that it was just a matter of making the beginning, of founding the first chapels, dreaming up the rituals of the cult, surrounding himself with the scientific talent necessary to realize his goals. Was there a touch of paranoia in his purpose, a bit of Hitler, a tinge of Napoleon, a tincture of Genghis Khan? Perhaps. Vorst complacently viewed himself as a fanatic and even as a megalomaniac. But a cool, rational megalomanic, and a successful one. He had been willing to stop at nothing to gain his ends, and he was just enough of a precog to know that he was going to gain them.

He said, "It's a big responsibility, setting out to transform the world. A man has to be a little daft to attempt it or even to think he can attempt it. But it helps to know what the outcome must be. One doesn't feel so idiotic, knowing that he's simply acting out the inevitable."

"It takes the challenge out of life," said the esper.

"Ah, Delphine, you touch the gaping wound! But you'd know, of course. How dreary it is to be playing out your own script, aware of what's ahead. At least I've had the mercy of uncertainty in the small things. I can't see very much myself, so I have to hitchhike with floaters like you, and the visions aren't clear. But you see clearly, don't you, Delphine? You've been along your own world-line. Have you seen your own burnout yet, Delphine?"

The esper's cheeks colored. She looked at the floor and did not answer.

"I'm sorry, Delphine," Vorst said. "I had no right to ask that. I retract it. Turn on for me, Delphine. Do your trick. Take me along. I've said too much today."

Shyly, the girl composed herself for her great effort. She had more control than most of her kind, Vorst knew. Whereas most of the precogs eventually slipped their moorings, Delphine had clung to her powers and her life and had reached what was, for her kind of esper, a ripe old age. She would burn out, too, one day, when she over-reached herself. But up to now she had been invaluable to Vorst, his crystal ball, the most helpful of all the floaters who had aided him in plotting his course. And if she could hold out just a while longer, until he saw his route past the final obstacles, the long journey would end and they both could rest.

She released her grip on the present and moved into that realm where all moments are now.

Vorst watched and waited and felt the girl taking him along as she began her time-shuttling. He could not initiate the journey himself, but he could follow. Mists enfolded him, and he swung dizzily along the line of time, as he had done so often before. He saw himself, here and here and here, and saw others, shadow-figures, dream-figures, lurking behind the curtains of time.

Lazarus? Yes, Lazarus was there. Kirby, too. Mondschein. All of them, the pawns in the game. Vorst saw the glow of otherness and looked out upon a landscape that was neither Earth nor Mars nor Venus. He trembled. He looked up at a tree eight hundred feet high, with a corona of azure leaves against a foggy sky. Then he was ripped away, and hurled into the stinking confusion of a rain-spattered city street, and stood before one of his early chapels. The building was on fire in the rain, and the smell of scorched wet wood assailed his nostrils. And then, smiling into the stunned, parched face of Reynolds Kirby. And then—

The sense of motion left him. He slipped back into his own matrix of time, making the adrenal adjustments that compensated for his exertions. The floater lay slumped in her chair, sweat-flecked, dazed. Vorst summoned an acolyte.

"Take her to her ward," he said. "Have them work on her until she comes back to her strength."

The acolyte nodded and lifted the girl. Vorst sat motionless until they were gone. He was satisfied with the session. It had confirmed his own intuitive ideas of his immediate direction, and that was always comforting.

"Send me Capodimonte," Vorst said into the communicator.

The chubby blue-robed figure entered a few minutes later. When Vorst was in Santa Fe, one did not waste time in getting to his quarters after a summons. Capodimonte was the District Supervisor for the Santa Fe region, and was customarily in charge here except when such figures as Vorst or Kirby were in residence. Capodimonte was stolid, loyal, useful. Vorst trusted him for delicate assignments. They exchanged quick, casual benedictions now.

Then Vorst said, "Capo, how long would it take you to pick the personnel for an interstellar expedition?"

"Inter—"

"Say, for departure later this year. Run the specs off at Archives and get together a few possible teams."

Capodimonte had recovered his aplomb. "What size teams?"

"All sizes. From two persons to about a dozen. Start with an Adam-and-Eve pair, and work up to, say, six couples. Matched for health, adaptability, compatibility, skills, and fertility."

"Espers?"

"With caution. You can throw in a couple of empaths, a couple of healers. Stay away from the exotics, though. And remember that these people are supposed to be pioneers. They've got to be flexible. We can do without geniuses on this trip, Capo."

"You want me to report to you or to Kirby when I've made the lists?"

"To me, Capo. I don't want you to utter a syllable about this to Kirby or anyone else. Just get in there and run off the groups as we've already programmed them. I'm not sure what size expedition we'll be sending, and I want to have a group ready that'll be self-sufficient at any level—two, four, eight, whatever it turns out to be. Take two or three days. When you've done that, put half a dozen of your best men to work on the logistics of the trip. Assume an esper-powered capsule and go over the optimum designs. We've had decades to plan it; we must have a whole arsenal full of blueprints. Look them over. This is your baby, Capo."

"Sir? One subversive question, please?"

"Ask it."

"Is this a hypothetical exercise I'm doing, or is this the real thing?"

"I don't know," said Vorst.

four

The blue face of a Venusian looked out of the screen, alien and forbidding, but its owner had been born an Earthman, and the terrestrial heritage betrayed itself in the shape of the skull, the set of the lips, the thrust of the chin. The face was that of David Lazarus, founder and resurrected head of the cult of Transcendent Harmony. Vorst had conferred often with Lazarus in the twelve years since the arch-heresiarch's resurrection. And always the two prophets had allowed themselves the luxury of full visual contact. It was monumentally expensive to bounce not only voices but images down the chain of relay stations that led from Venus to Earth, but expense meant little to these men. Vorst insisted. He liked to see Lazarus's transformed face as they spoke. It gave him something to focus on during the long, dull time-lags in their conversations. Even at the speed of light it took a while for a message to get from planet to planet. Even a simple exchange of views required more than an hour.

Comfortable in his nest of webfoam, Vorst said, "I think it's time to unite our movements, David. We complement one another. There's nothing to gain from further division."

"There might be something to lose by union," said Lazarus. "We're the younger branch. If you reabsorbed us, we'd be swallowed up in your hierarchy."

"Not so. I guarantee you that your Harmonists will remain fully autonomous. More than that, I'll guarantee you a dominant role in policy setting."

"What kind of guarantee can you offer?"

"Let that pass a moment," Vorst said. "I've got an interstellar team ready to go. They'll be fully equipped in a matter of months. I mean *fully* equipped. They'll be able to cope with anything they meet. But they have to have a way of getting out of the solar system. Give us a push, David. You've got the personnel now. We've monitored your experiments."

Lazarus nodded, his gill-bunches quivering. "I won't deny what we've done. We can push a thousand tons from here to Pluto. We can keep the same mass going right to infinity."

"How long to get to Pluto?"

"Fast. I won't tell you exactly how fast. But let's just say the stars are in reach. Have been for the past eight or ten months. We could get a ship there in—oh, let's call it a year. Of course, we'd have no way of maintaining contact. We can push, but we can't talk across a dozen light-years. Can you?"

"No," said Vorst. "The expedition would be out of contact the moment it got past radio range. It would have to send back a conventional relay ship to announce its safe arrival. We wouldn't know for decades. But we have to try. Give us your men, David."

"You realize it would burn out dozens of our most promising youngsters?"

"I realize. Give us your men, anyway. We understand techniques for repairing burnouts. Let them push the ship to the stars, and when they drop in their tracks, we'll try to fix them up again. That's what Santa Fe is for."

"First drive them to exhaustion, then patch them together?" Lazarus asked. "That's ruthless. Are the stars that important? I'd rather see these boys develop their powers here on Venus and remain intact."

"We need them."

"So do we."

Vorst made use of the interval to flood his body with stimulants. He was tingling, palpitating with vigor by the time his reply was due. He said, "David, I own you. I made you and I want you. I put you to sleep in 2090 when you were nothing, an upstart, and I brought you back to life in 2152 and gave you a world. You owe me everything. Now I'm calling in that obligation. I've been waiting a hundred years to reach this position. You people finally have the espers who can send my people to the stars. Whatever the personal cost at your end, I want you to send them."

The strain of that speech left Vorst dizzy with fatigue. But he had time to recover. Time to think, to wait for the reply. He had made his gamble, and now it was up to Lazarus. Vorst did not have many cards left to play.

The blue-faced figure in the screen was motionless; Vorst's words had not even reached Venus yet. Lazarus's reply was a long time in coming.

He said, "I didn't think you'd be so blunt, Vorst. Why should I be grateful to you for reviving me, when you jammed me into that hole in the first place? Oh, I know. Because my movement was insignificant when you took me away from it and a major force when you brought me back. Do you take credit for that, too?" A pause. "Never mind. I don't want to give you my espers. Breed your own, if you want to get to the stars."

"You're talking foolishness. You want the stars, too, David. But you don't have the technical facilities, up there in the backwoods, to equip an expedition. I do. Let's join forces. It's what you yourself want to do, no matter how tough you talk now. Let me tell you what's holding you back from agreeing to join me, David. You're afraid of what your own people will do to you when they find out you've agreed to cooperate. They'll say you've sold out to the Vorsters. You're frozen in a position you don't believe, just because you don't have real independence. Assert yourself, David. Use your powers. I put that planet into your hands. Now I want you to repay me."

"How can I go to Mondschein and Martell and the others and tell them that I've meekly agreed to submit to you?" Lazarus asked. "They're restless enough at having had a resurrected martyr slapped down on top of them. There are times when I expect them to martyr me again, and this time for good. I need a bargaining point."

Vorst smiled. Victory was in his grasp now.

He said, "Tell them, David, that I offer you supreme authority over both worlds. Tell them that the Brotherhood not only will welcome the Harmonists back, but that you'll be made the sole head of both branches of the faith."

"Both?"

"Both."

"And what becomes of you?"

Vorst told him. And once the words were past his lips, the Founder sank back, limp with relief, knowing that he had made the final move in a game a century old, and that it had all come out in the right way.

five

Reynolds Kirby was with his therapist when the summons came to go to Vorst. The Hemispheric Coordinator lay in a nutrient bath, an adapted Nothing Chamber whose purpose was not oblivion but revivification. If Kirby had chosen to escape into temporary nothingness, he could have sealed himself off from the universe and entered complete suspension. He had long since outgrown the need for such amusements, though. Now he was content to loll in the nutrient bath, restoring the vital substances after a fatiguing day, while an esper therapist combed the snags from his soul.

Ordinarily, Kirby did not tolerate interruptions of such sessions. At his age he needed all the peace he could get. He had been born too early to share the quasi-immortality of the younger generations; his body could not snap back to vitality the way a twenty-second-century man's body could, for he had not had the benefit of a century of Vorster research when he was born. There was one exception to Kirby's rule, however: a summons from Vorst took precedence over everything, even a session of needed therapy.

The therapist knew it. Deftly he brought the session to a premature close and fortified Kirby for his return to the tensions of the world. In less than half an hour the Coordinator was on his way to the white dome-roofed building where Vorst made his headquarters.

Vorst looked shaky. Kirby had never seen the Founder

look so drained of strength. The vault of Vorst's forehead was like the roof of a skull, and the dark eyes blazed with a peculiarly discomfiting intensity. A low pumping sound was evident in the room: Vorst's machinery, feeding strength to the ancient body. Kirby took the seat toward which Vorst beckoned him. Strong fingers in the upholstery grasped him and began to knead the tension out of him.

Vorst said, "I'll be calling a council meeting in a little while to ratify the steps I've just taken. But before the entire group gathers, I want to discuss things with you, run them through once or twice."

Kirby's expression was guarded. After decades with Vorst, he could supply an instant translation: *I've done something authoritarian,* Vorst was saying, *and I'm going to call in everybody to rubber-stamp an okay on it, but first I'm going to force a rubber-stamping out of you.* Kirby was prepared to acquiesce in whatever Vorst had done. He was not a weak man by nature, but one did not dispute the doings of Vorst. The last one who had seriously attempted to try was Lazarus, who had slept in a box on Mars for sixty years as a result.

Into Kirby's wary silence Vorst murmured, "I've talked to Lazarus and closed the deal. He's agreed to supply us with pushers, as many as we need. It's possible we'll have an interstellar expedition on its way by the end of the year."

"I feel a little numb at that, Noel."

"Anticlimactic, isn't it? For a hundred years you move an inch at a time toward that goal, and suddenly you find yourself staring at the finish line, and the thrill of pursuit becomes the boredom of accomplishment."

"We haven't landed that expedition on another solar system yet," Kirby reminded the Founder quietly.

"We will. We will. That's beyond doubt. We're at the finish line now. Capodimonte's already running personnel checks for the expedition. We'll be outfitting the capsule soon. Lazarus's bunch will cooperate, and off we'll go. That much is certain."

"How did you get him to agree, Noel?"

"By showing him how it will be after the expedition has

set out. Tell me, have you given much thought to the goals of the Brotherhood once we've sent that first expedition?"

Kirby hesitated. "Well—sending more expeditions, I guess. And consolidating our position. Continuing the medical research. Carrying on with all our current work."

"Exactly. A long smooth slide toward utopia. No longer an uphill climb. That's why I won't stay around to run things any longer."

"What?"

"I'm going on the expedition," Vorst said.

If Vorst had ripped off one of his limbs and clubbed him to the floor with it, Kirby would not have been more amazed. The Founder's words hit him with an almost physical jolt, making him recoil. Kirby seized the arms of his chair, and in response the chair seized him, cradling him gently until his spasm of shock abated.

"*You're* going?" Kirby blurted. "No. No. It's beyond belief, Noel. It's madness."

"My mind's made up. My work on Earth is done. I've guided the Brotherhood for a century, and that's long enough. I've seen it take control of Earth, and by proxy I have Venus, too, and I have the cooperation if not exactly the support of the Martians. I've done all I've intended to do here. With the departure of the first interstellar expedition, I will have fulfilled what I'll be so gaudy as to call my mission on Earth. It's time to be moving along. I'll try another solar system."

"We won't let you go," Kirby said, astounded by his own words. "You can't go! At your age—to get aboard a capsule bound for—"

"If I don't go," said Vorst, "there will be no capsule bound for anywhere."

"Don't talk that way, Noel. You sound like a spoiled child threatening to call the party off if we don't play the game your way. There are others bound up in the Brotherhood, too."

To Kirby's surprise, Vorst looked merely amused at the harsh accusation. "I think you're misinterpreting my words," he said. "I don't mean to say that unless I go along, *I'll* halt the expedition. I mean that the use of Lazarus's espers is contingent on my leaving. If I'm not aboard that capsule, he won't lend his pushers."

For the second time in ten minutes Kirby was rocked by amazement. This time there was pain, too, for he was aware that there had been a betrayal.

"Is that the deal you made, Noel?"

"It was a fair price to pay. A shift of power is long overdue. I step out of the picture; Lazarus becomes supreme head of the movement; you can be his vicar on Earth. We get the espers. We open the sky. It works well for everybody concerned."

"No, Noel."

"I'm weary of being here. I want to leave. Lazarus wants me to leave, too. I'm too big, I overtop the entire movement. It's time for mortals to move in. You and Lazarus can divide the authority. He'll have the spiritual supremacy, but you'll run Earth. The two of you will work out some kind of communicant relation between the Harmonists and the Brotherhood. It won't be too hard; the rituals are similar enough. Ten years and any lingering bitterness will be gone. And I'll be a dozen light-years away, safely out of your path, unable to meddle, living in retirement. Out to pasture on World X of System Y. Yes?"

"I don't believe any of this, Noel. That you'd abdicate after a century, go swooshing off to nowhere with a bunch of pioneers, live in a log cabin on an unknown planet at the age of nearly a hundred and fifty, drop the reins—"

"Start believing it," said Vorst. For the first time in the conversation the old whiplash tone returned to his voice. "I'm going. It's decided. In a sense, I *have* gone."

"What does that mean?"

"You know I'm a very low-order floater. That I plan things by hitchhiking with precogs."

"Yes."

"I've seen the outcome. I know how it was, and so I know how it's going to be. I leave. I've followed the plan this far—followed and led, all in one, heels over head through time. Everything I've done I've had a hint of beforehand. From founding the Brotherhood right to this moment. So it's settled. I go."

Kirby closed his eyes. He struggled for balance.

Vorst said, "Look back on the path I've traveled. Was there a false step anywhere? The Brotherhood prospered. It took Earth. When we were strong enough to afford a schism, I encouraged the Harmonist heresy."

"*You* encouraged—"

"I chose Lazarus for what he had to do and filled him full of ideas. He was just an insignificant acolyte, clay in my hands. That's why you never knew him in the early days. But he was there. I took him. I molded him. I got his movement going in opposition to ours."

"Why, Noel?"

"It didn't pay to be monolithic. I was hedging my bets. The Brotherhood was designed to win Earth, and it did, but the same principles didn't—couldn't—appeal to Venus. So I started a second cult. I tailored that one for Venus and gave them Lazarus. Later I gave them Mondschein, too. Do you remember that, in 2095? He was only a greedy little acolyte, but I saw the strength in him, and I nudged him around until he found himself a changed one on Venus. I built that entire organization."

"And you knew that they'd come up with pushers?" Kirby asked incredulously.

"I didn't know. I hoped. All I knew was that setting up the Harmonists was a good idea, because I saw that it *had been* a good idea. Follow? For the same reason I took Lazarus away and hid him in a crypt for sixty years. I didn't know why at the time. But I knew it might be useful to keep the Harmonist martyr in my pocket for a while, as a card to play in the future. I played that card twelve years ago, and since then the Harmonists have been mine. Today I played my last card: myself. I have to leave. My work is done, anyway. I'm bored with running out the skein. I've juggled everything for a hundred years, setting up my own opposition, creating conflicts designed to lead to an ultimate synthesis, and that synthesis is here, and I'm leaving."

After a long silence Kirby said, "You humiliate me, Noel, by asking me to ratify a decision that's already as immutable as the tides and the sunrise."

"You're free to oppose it at the council meeting."

"But you'll go, anyway?"

"Yes. I'd like your support, though. It won't matter to the eventual outcome, but I'd still rather have you on my side than not. I'd like to think that you of all people understand what I've been doing all these years. Do you believe there's any reason for me to stay on Earth any longer?"

"We need you, Noel. That's the only reason."

"Now you're the one who's being childish. You don't need me. The plan is fulfilled. It's time to clear out and turn the job over to others. You're too dependent on me, Ron. You can't get used to the idea that I'm not going to be pulling the strings forever."

"Perhaps that's it," admitted Kirby. "But whose fault is that? You've surrounded yourself with yes-men. You've made yourself indispensable. Here you sit at the heart of the movement like a sacred fire, and none of us can get close enough to be singed. Now you're taking the fire away."

"Transferring it," said Vorst. "Here, I've got a job for you. The members of the council will be arriving in six hours. I'm going to make my announcement, and I suppose it'll shake everybody else the way it shook you. Go off by yourself for the next six hours and think about all I've just said. Reconcile yourself to it. More, don't just accept it, but *approve* of it. At the meeting stand up and explain not simply why it's all right if I go, but why it's necessary and vital to the future of the Brotherhood that I go."

"You mean—"

"Don't say anything now. You're still hostile. You won't be after you've examined the dynamics of it. Keep your mouth closed till then."

Kirby smiled. "You're still pulling strings, aren't you?"

"It's an old habit by now. But this is the last one I'll

ever pull. And I promise you, your mind will change. You'll see my point of view in an hour or two. By nightfall you'll be willing to stuff me in that capsule yourself. I know you will. I know you."

six

In a leafy glade on Venus, the pushers were at their sport.

An avenue of vast trees unrolled toward the pearly horizon. Their jagged leaves met overhead to form a thick canopy. Below, on the muddy, fungus-dotted ground, a dozen Venusian boys with bluish skins and green robes exercised their abilities. At a distance several larger figures watched them. David Lazarus stood in the center of the group. About him were the Harmonist leaders: Christopher Mondschein, Nicholas Martell, Claude Emory.

Lazarus had been through a great deal at the hands of these men. To them, he had been only a name in a martyrology, a revered and unreal figure by whose absent power they governed a creed. They had had to adjust to his return, and it had not been easy. There had been a time when Lazarus thought they would put him to death. That time was past now, and they abided by his wishes. But, because he had slept so long, he was at once younger and older than his lieutenants, and sometimes that interfered with the exercising of his full authority.

He said, "It's settled. Vorst will leave and the schism will end. I'll work something out with Kirby."

"It's a trap," said Emory gloomily. "Keep away from it, David. Vorst can't be trusted."

"Vorst brought me back to life."

"Vorst put you in that crypt in the first place," Emory insisted. "You said so yourself."

"We can't be sure of that," Lazarus replied, though it

was true that Vorst himself had admitted the act to him in their last conversation. "We're only guessing. There's no evidence that—"

Mondschein broke in, "We don't have any reason to trust Vorst, Claude. But if he's really and verifiably aboard that capsule, what do we have to lose by pushing him to Betelgeuse or Procyon? We're rid of him, and we'll be dealing with Kirby. Kirby's a reasonable man. None of that damnable superdeviousness about him."

"It's too pat," Emory insisted. "Why should a man with Vorst's power just step down voluntarily?"

"Perhaps he's bored," said Lazarus. "There's something about absolute power that can't be understood except by someone who holds it. It's dull. You can enjoy moving and shaking the world for twenty years, thirty, fifty—but Vorst's been on top for a hundred. He wants to move along. I say take the offer. We're well rid of him, and we can handle Kirby. Besides, he's got a good point: neither his side nor ours can get to the stars without the help of the other. I'm for it. It's worth the try."

Nicholas Martell gestured toward the pushers. "We'll lose some of them, don't forget. You can't push a capsule to the stars without overloading the pushers."

"Vorst has offered rehabilitation services," said Lazarus.

"One other point," Mondschein remarked. "Under the new agreement, we'd have access to Vorster hospitals ourselves. Just as a purely selfish matter, I'd like that. I think the time has come to turn away from haughtiness and give in to Vorst. He's willing to check out. All right. Let him go, and look for our own advantage with Kirby."

Lazarus smiled. He had not hoped to win Mondschein's support that easily. But Mondschein was old, past ninety, and he was hungry for the care that Vorster medics could give him, care that was not to be had on rugged Venus. Monschein had seen the Santa Fe hospitals himself when he was a young man, and he knew what miracles they could perform. It was not a terribly worthy motive, thought Lazarus. But it was a human motive, at least, and

Mondschein was human behind his gills and blued skin. *So are we all,* Lazarus realized. *Though they aren't.*

He looked toward the pushers. They were fifth- and sixth-generation Venusians. The seed of Earth was in them, but they were far removed from the original stock. The genetic manipulations that had first adapted mankind for life on Venus bred true; these boys were something other than human by this time. They were intent on their games. It was little effort for them to transport objects great distances now. They could send each other around Venus virtually instantaneously, or hurl a boulder to Earth in an hour or two. What they could not do was transport themselves, for they needed a fulcrum to do their pushing with. But that was minor! They could not flit from place to place on the strength of their own powers, but they could thrust each other about.

Lazarus watched them: appearing, disappearing, lifting, throwing. Only children, not yet in full command of their powers. What strengths would be theirs when they were fully mature, he wondered?

And how many would die to send mankind beyond his present boundaries?

A saw-winged bird, faintly luminous in the midday dusk, shot diagonally across the sky just above the treetop canopy. One of the young pushers looked up, grinned, caught the bird and sent it whirling half a mile through the clouds. A squawk of rage, distant but audible, filtered back.

Lazarus said, "The deal is closed. We help Vorst, and Vorst goes. Done?"

"Done," said Mondschein quickly.

"Done," Martell murmured, scuffing at the grayish moss that festooned the ground.

"Claude?" Lazarus asked.

Emory scowled. He peered at a long-limbed boy, returning from a jaunt to some other continent, who materialized no more than six yards away. Emory's narrow-featured face looked dark with tension.

"Done," he said.

seven

The capsule was an obelisk of beryllium steel, fifty feet high, an uncertain ark to send across the sea of stars. It contained living quarters for eleven, a computer of uncomfortably awe-inspiring abilities, and a subminiaturized treasury of all that was worth salvaging from two billion years of life on Earth.

"Prepare the capsule," Vorst had instructed Brother Capodimonte, "as though the sun were going nova next month and we had to save what was important."

As a former anthropologist, Capodimonte had his own ideas about the contents of such an ark, but he kept them separate from his concept of what Vorst required. Quietly, a subcommittee of Brothers had planned the interstellar expedition on a someday-far-away basis decades ago, and had replanned it several times, so that Capodimonte had the benefit of the thinking of other men. That was a comfort to him.

There were troublesome elements of mystery about the project. He did not, for example, know the nature of the world to which the pioneers were bound. No one did. There was no telling, at this distance, whether it really could harbor Terran-style life.

Astronomers had found hundreds of planets scattered through other systems. Some could dimly be picked up by telescopic sensors; others could only be inferred from computations of disturbed stellar orbits. But the planets were there. Would they welcome Earthmen?

Only one planet out of nine in Earth's own system was

naturally habitable—not a cheering prognosis for other systems. It had taken two generations of hard work to Terraform Mars; the eleven pioneers would hardly be able to do that. It had taken the highest genetic skills to convert men into Venusians; that, too, would be beyond the range of the voyagers. They would have to find a suitable world, or fail.

Espers in the Santa Fe retinue said that suitable worlds existed. They had peered into the heavens, reached forth their minds, made contact with tangible and habitable planets out there. Illusion? Deception? Capodimonte was in no position to determine that.

Reynolds Kirby, troubled by the project from first to last, said to Capodimonte, "Is it true that they don't even know what star they'll be aiming for?"

"That's true. They've detected some kind of emanations coming from somewhere. Don't ask me how. The way this thing is planned, our espers will supply the guidance and their pushers will supply the propulsion. We find, they heave."

"A voyage to anywhere?"

"To anywhere," Capodimonte agreed. "They rip a hole in the sky and shove the capsule through. It doesn't travel through normal space, whatever normal space is. It lands on this world that our espers claim to have connected with out there, and they send a message back, telling us where they are. We get the message about a generation from now. But meanwhile we'll have sent other expeditions. A one-way journey to nowhere. And Vorst is the first to take it."

Kirby shook his head. "It's hard to believe, isn't it? But evidently it's going to be a success."

"Oh?"

"Yes. Vorst's had his floaters out there looking, you see. They tell him that he arrived safely. So he's willing to step out into the dark, because he knows in advance that he's not running any risks."

"Do you believe that?" asked Capodimonte, shuffling through his inventory sheets.

"No."

Neither did Brother Capodimonte. But he did not quarrel with the role assigned to him. He had been at the council meeting where Vorst had announced his stunning intention, and he had heard Reynolds Kirby rise and eloquently argue the case for allowing the Founder to depart. Kirby's thesis had been a sound one, within the context of nightmare that this whole project embraced. And so the capsule would leave, powered by the joint efforts of some blue-skinned boys, and guided on a thread through the heavens by the roving minds of Brotherhood espers, and Noel Vorst would never walk the Earth again.

Capodimonte checked his lists.

Food.

Clothing.

Books.

Tools.

Medical equipment.

Communication devices.

Weapons.

Power sources.

The expedition, Capodimonte thought, would be adequately furnished for its adventure. The whole thing might be madness, or it might be the grandest enterprise ever attempted by man; Brother Capodimonte could not tell which. But one thing was certain: the expedition would be adequately furnished. He had seen to that.

eight

It was the day of departure. Chill winter winds raked New Mexico on this late-December day. The capsule stood in a desert flat a dozen miles from the inner compound of the Santa Fe research center. From here to the horizon it was a wilderness of sagebrush and juniper and piñon pine, and in the distance the bowl of mountains rose. Though he was well insulated, Reynolds Kirby shivered as the wind assailed the plateau. In another few days the year 2165 would be dawning, but Noel Vorst would not be here to welcome it. Kirby was not accustomed to that idea yet.

The pushers from Venus had arrived a week ago. There were twenty of them, and since it was inconvenient for them to live in breathing-suits all their time on Earth, the Vorsters had erected a little bit of Venus for them. A domed building not far from the capsule housed them; it was pumped full of the poisonous muck that they were accustomed to breathing. Lazarus and Mondschein had come with them and were under the dome now, getting everything prepared.

Mondschein would remain after the event, to undergo an overhauling in Santa Fe. Lazarus was going back to Venus in a couple of days. But first he and Kirby would face each other across a conference table and hammer out the basic clauses of the new entente. They had met once, twelve years ago, but not for long. Since Lazarus's arrival on Earth, Kirby had spoken briefly to him and had come away with the feeling that the Harmonist prophet, though strong-willed and purposeful, would not be difficult ultimately to reach understandings with. He hoped not.

Now, on the wintry plateau, the high leaders of the Brotherhood of the Immanent Radiance were gathering to watch their leader vanish. Kirby, glancing around, saw Capodimonte and Magnus and Ashton and Langholt and all the others, dozens of them, spiraling down the echelons into the middle levels of the organization. They were all watching him. They could not watch Vorst, for Vorst was in the capsule already, along with the other members of the expedition. Five men, five women, and Vorst. All of the others under forty, healthy, capable, resilient. And Vorst. The Founder's quarters aboard the capsule were comfortable, but it was lunacy to think of that old man plunging into the universe like this.

Supervisor Magnus, the European Coordinator, stepped to Kirby's side. He was a small, sharp-featured man who, like most of the other leaders of the Brotherhood, had served in its ranks for more than seventy years.

"He's actually going," Magnus said.

"Soon. Yes. No doubt of it."

"Did you speak to him this morning?"

"Briefly," Kirby said. "He seems very calm."

"He seemed very calm when he blessed us last night," said Magnus. "Almost joyful."

"He's putting down a great burden. You'd be joyful, too, if you could be translated into the sky and shrug off your responsibilities."

Magnus said, "I wish we could prevent this."

Kirby turned and looked bluntly at the little man. "This is a necessary thing," he said. "It must happen, or the movement will founder of its own success."

"I heard your speech before the council, yes, but—"

"We've reached the fulfillment level of our first evolutionary stage," said Kirby. "Now we need to extend our mythology. Symbolically, Vorst's departure is invaluable to us. He ascends into the sky, leaving us to carry on his work and go on to new purposes. If he remained, we'd begin to mark time. Now we can use his glorious example to inspire us. With Vorst leading the way to the new worlds, we who remain can build on the foundation he bequeaths us."

"You sound as though you believed it."

"I do," said Kirby. "I didn't at first. But Vorst was right. He said I'd understand why he was going, and I came to see it. He's ten times as valuable to the movement doing this as he would be if he remained."

Magnus murmured, "He isn't content to be Christ and Mohammed. He has to be Moses, too, and also Elijah."

"I never thought I'd hear you speak of him so coarsely," said Kirby.

"I never did either," Magnus replied. "Damn it, I don't want him to go!"

Kirby was astonished to see tears glistening in Magnus's pale eyes.

"That's precisely why he's leaving," Kirby said, and then both men were silent.

Capodimonte moved toward them. "Everything's ready," he announced. "I've got the word from Lazarus that the pushers are in series."

"What about our guidance people?" Kirby asked.

"They've been ready for an hour."

Kirby looked toward the gleaming capsule. "Might as well get it over with, then."

"Yes," Capodimonte said. "Might as well."

Lazarus, Kirby knew, was waiting for a signal from him. From now on, *all* signals would come from him, at least on Earth. But that thought no longer disturbed him. He had adjusted to the situation. He was in command.

Symbolic regalia cluttered the field—Harmonist ikons, a big cobalt reactor, the paraphernalia of both the cults that now were merging. Kirby gestured to an acolyte, and moderator rods were withdrawn. The reactor surged into life.

The Blue Fire danced high above the reactor, and its glow stained the hull of the capsule. Cold light, Cerenkov radiation, the Vorster symbol, sparkled on the plateau, and all through the watching multitude ran the sounds of devotion, the whispered litanies, the murmured recapitulations of the stations of the spectrum. While the man who had devised those words sat hidden within the walls of that teardrop of steel in the center of the gathering.

The flare of the Blue Fire was the signal to the Venusians in their nearby dome. Now was their moment to gather their power and hurl the capsule outward, planting man's hand on a new world in the stars.

"What are they waiting for?" Magnus asked querulously.

"Maybe it won't happen," said Capodimonte.

Kirby said nothing. And then it began to happen.

nine

Kirby had not quite known what to expect. In his fantasies of the scene he had pictured a dozen capering Venusians dancing around the capsule, holding hands, their foreheads bulging with the effort of lifting the vehicle and hurling it out of the world. But the Venusians were nowhere to be seen; they were off in their dome, several hundred yards away, and Kirby suspected that they were neither holding hands nor showing outward signs of strain.

In his reveries, too, he had imagined the capsule taking off the way a rocket would, rising a few feet from the ground, wobbling a bit, rising a little more, suddenly soaring up, crossing the sky on a potent trajectory, dwindling, vanishing from sight at last. But that was not the way it was really to be, either.

He waited. A long moment passed.

He thought of Vorst, making landfall on some other world. An inhabited world, perhaps? What would be Vorst's impact when he came to that virgin territory? Vorst was an irresistible force, terrifying and unique. Wherever he went, he would transform all that was about him. Kirby felt sorry for the ten hapless pioneers who would have the benefit of Vorst's immediate guidance. He wondered what kind of colony they would build.

Whatever it was, it would succeed. Success was in Vorst's nature. He was hideously old, but he had frightening vitality still locked within him. The Founder seemed to relish the challenge of beginning anew. Kirby wished him well.

"There they go," Capodimonte whispered.

It was true. The capsule was still on the ground, but now the air about it wavered, as though stirred by heat waves rising from the parched, sandy soil.

Then the capsule was gone.

That was all. Kirby stared at the empty place where it had been. Vorst had been taken up into the heavens, and a gateway to somewhere had been opened.

"There is a Oneness from which all life stems," someone said gently behind Kirby. "The infinite variety of the universe we owe to—"

Another voice said, "Man and woman, star and stone, tree and bird—"

Another said, "In the strength of the spectrum, the quantum, and the holy angstrom—"

Kirby did not remain to listen to the familiar prayers, nor did he pray himself. He looked briefly at the bareness in the desert once more, and then upward at the harsh blue sky, already deepening toward nightfall. It was done. Vorst was gone, his scheming ended so far as Earth was concerned, and now it was the turn of lesser men. The way was open. Humanity could spill out across the heavens. Perhaps. Perhaps.

Alone in this great assembly of the faithful, Kirby turned his back on the now sacred spot from which Vorst had made his ascent. Very slowly, a tall figure whose late-afternoon shadow stretched for yards, Kirby walked away from the place where Noel Vorst had been, and toward the place where David Lazarus was waiting to speak with him.

ABOUT THE AUTHOR

Robert Silverberg was born in New York and makes his home in the San Francisco area. He has written several hundred science fiction stories and over seventy science fiction novels. He has won two Hugo awards and four Nebula awards. He is a past president of the Science Fiction Writers of America. Silverberg's other Bantam titles include *Lord Valentine's Castle, Majipoor Chronicles, The Book of Skulls, The World Inside, Thorns, The Masks of Time, Dying Inside, Downward to the Earth, Tower of Glass, Valentine Pontifex,* and *World of a Thousand Colors.*